DARK MINDS PRESS

Slaughter Beach

Published by

Dark Minds Press

31 Gristmill Close

Cheltenham

Glos.

GL51 0PZ

www.darkmindspress.com

Mail@darkmindspress.com

First Print Edition - October 2015

Cover Image © 77studios

www.77studios.blogspot.com

The copyright of this story

remains the property of the author.

Edited and typeset by Anthony Watson

ISBN-13: 978-1516969708

ISBN-10: 1516969707

DARK MINDS NOVELLAS

1

INTRODUCTION

Ben Jones knows a lot of stuff. I mean really, a lot of stuff. This is a good thing. It's good because when I'm writing and need some technical information about what a Russian sniper would wear or what kind of bullets an ex-American Civil War soldier would put in his rifle then I know I can send an email to him and he'll tell me – and provide lots of other information that I can use in the story besides.

It's also good because as well as this encyclopaedic knowledge, Ben also has a vivid imagination and is able to combine the two with his great skill as a writer to produce entertaining, realistic stories which are a joy to read.

He doesn't limit himself to just one genre either. He has had numerous short stories published in the fields of horror, war, western and crime – his debut novel, *Pennies for Charon*, falls into the latter category and features his character Charlie Bars – and it's with some degree of pleasure and pride that here at Dark Minds Press we'll be publishing his collection of weird westerns, *Ride the Dark Country* in the not too distant future. A sample of one of the stories is included at the end of this book.

And so to *Slaughter Beach*. This is out and out horror, firmly in the tradition of the slasher/exploitation films and books whose lurid covers graced many a VHS box and dustcover back in the seventies and eighties. It's set *in* the seventies and those days are recreated vividly here. Also created vividly are some particularly gruesome death scenes, which are certainly not for the faint-hearted. It's a potent blend of sex, drugs and mayhem which cracks along at breakneck speed.

So brace yourselves and enjoy the ride. And do remember to breathe in every now and then…

Anthony Watson, August 2015

SLAUGHTER BEACH

-Where paradise becomes a
blood drenched hell-

A novella

By

Benedict J Jones

To Fran, for "ploughing on…"

"It is with much embarrassment, but I have returned."

– Shoichi Yokoi

1.

The beer did little to cool Don Curtis in the sweat-box of a bar in which he was sitting. He looked up and watched the large ceiling fan rotate slowly. It wasn't so much the heat as it was the humidity, just walking across the room felt like moving through cotton wool. But Curtis had no intention of moving from the table he sat at. On a small stage the stripper, a brown skinned island girl, didn't even bother to do any more than step from foot to foot in some kind of time to David Soul's *Don't Give Up On Us* and Curtis found himself envying her lack of clothes. He lit a cigarette and gestured for another beer just as the door opened and a fat, red faced, man in a crumpled white suit fell into the bar. The fat man made it as far as Don's table where he collapsed into a chair.

"Better make that two beers, Mike."

The barman nodded and broke the neck on another cold one. The fat man caught his breath and nodded his thanks to Curtis before wiping a handkerchief across his forehead. He was in his early fifties, nearly twenty years older than Curtis, but he was the only other Australian in town so they had fallen in together in an easy expatriate camaraderie.

"I swear this place will be the death of me."

"Keep running about like a blue-arsed fly and it will be."

"This is all on account of you."

"How d'you make that out, Clive?"

"There's a bloke looking to hire a boat – he's heard about you and wants to meet you."

"That so," mused Curtis, taking a deep bite out of his bottle.

Clive nodded.

"Down by your boat right now."

"Might go and see him in a bit."

Clive turned even redder.

"Like you don't need the money!"

Curtis smiled.

"I said I'll go and see him. Now stop being an old woman and enjoy your beer."

After sucking on his front teeth for a moment Clive took a long swallow and necked half of his bottle.

"Who's this fella looking at my boat?"

"A yank. Some photographer, apparently, wants to go to the islands up north. He says the remoter the better."

"What in the hell for?"

"I don't know. To take pictures I'd imagine. Jesus, Don, I'm not your bloody booking agent go and ask him yourself."

Curtis threw back the last of his beer and got up.

"Think I will. I'll catch you in a bit, Clive. Get him another beer, Mike – on me."

*

The walk from the bar down to the moorings where Curtis kept his boat, *The Ariadne*, was a short one but he took it slow, the sweat already beginning to show through the loose white shirt he wore. When he turned the corner to the moorings and saw his boat she brought a smile to his face, as she always did. *The Ariadne* was a converted US crash boat, an eighty five footer painted white to cover the US Navy grey. The crash boats were designed to help pick up pilots who had been forced to ditch in the sea but the advent of helicopters had scuttled their usage somewhat. She was a bit rusty but Curtis loved her like the wife he didn't have. He looked and saw a small knot of people standing near the jetty; a man and three women.

"Help you?" he called as he got closer.

A dark-haired man in small white shorts and a blue tennis jumper with a camera hanging around his neck turned to look at Curtis.

"You the captain?"

The accent was American, west coast Curtis reckoned. He nodded and took the cigarettes out of the pocket of his worn jeans. He lit one and then spoke.

"Yep, that's me."

"My name's William Marshall – maybe you've heard of me?"

"Don Curtis and no, I haven't - should I have?"

The man laughed and showed two rows of perfectly even white teeth.

"The brutal Australian honesty, I've heard about that."

Curtis shrugged.

"Heard you were interested in my boat?"

Marshall nodded.

"I want to charter it."

"Well, that's my business."

"What kind of boat is it?"

"Old US Navy crash boat, they used to pick up downed pilots but the boats kind of got superseded so they sold them off. She's had a conversion job done – comfortable for passengers and cargo."

"And do you know the far islands?"

"Sure, not much call to go out there but I know them well enough. Why do you want to go there?"

Marshall gestured at the Nikon hung around his neck and the bevy of women stood behind him all tall and long legged, with jutting hip bones and bee sting tits but there the similarity ended; one was blonde, one dark haired and olive skinned, the third was possibly the darkest skinned black woman Curtis had ever seen and the last had the hint of the Orient in her almond shaped green eyes. The way the women looked, their clothes, everything about them were out of place on the small backwater harbour. It was as though just by being there they made it even more drab and backwards.

"I'm a photographer. Brought some model friends out here and I've heard the outlying islands are stunning. We like to get off the beaten track, see the undiscovered world."

Curtis shrugged again.

"All the islands are beautiful."

That too-white smile again.

"But I'd like to go to the far islands. And I'll be footing the bill."

Curtis tossed off a salute.

"Then I'll call you sir and tell you we're setting out at first light. That way we'll be there by nightfall. Camp out on the beach and then you'll have a full day and another night before we head back. That sound okay to you?"

"Exactly what I had hoped for."

"Charter fee's payable up front. Just the five of you?"

Marshall took out a small leather zip case and opened it up.

"No there're three assistants I'll be bringing. Will we all fit in there alright?"

"I'd have thought so," replied Don.

"Good old US dollars okay?"

"Good as anything."

"Six hundred cover it?"

Don whistled.

"And then some. Want me to arrange some supplies with what's left over?"

"Yes, fine. What time do we cast off, Cap'n?"

Don gave him the eye for a moment as he pocketed the folded bills.

"Five. Early enough for you?"

Marshall smiled, whiter than Colombian pure, and nodded.

"Fine with us."

Don looked the tall skinny women over again and touched his forelock.

"Ladies."

2.

The supplies were stowed and *The Ariadne* was ready by a quarter to five. Curtis stood on the jetty and waited. He lit a cigarette and looked at the four man crew he had hired on. They were all locals that he had worked with before. Don had paid them thirty five dollars each, bought the supplies and paid off some debts. He still had the better part of a hundred dollars left in his pocket and that buoyed him.

"Where the fuck are they?" asked Samson, one of the local crew, a big man with a head of curly black hair that was starting to streak with grey.

"Fucked if I know," replied Curtis "still, it's their money."

Samson shrugged and lit a cigarette of his own. Curtis stepped back onto the boat and headed into the bridge house. He checked the charts for the third time and made sure the course was set to the outlying islands. He then made sure his bottle of rum was well stashed, wrapped in an old towel in the locked gun cabinet along with an M1 carbine and a .357 Ruger revolver. Pirates and thieves were rare but Curtis never liked to take chances, there wasn't much ammunition but he reckoned they could put up a pretty decent account for themselves if anyone tried to take his baby.

"Ahoy the ship!" came a shout from outside.

Curtis turned at the voice and hurried outside. He stopped and put his hands on his hips to survey the party that stood on the jetty; there was Marshall and the four tall models, along with them were a short dark woman in her mid-twenties and two men. One of the men was tall and bearded, the other short, skinny and clean shaven. There was a pile of travel cases and wooden boxes of wines and spirits.

"Get that aboard boys and get it stowed tight."

His four man crew swarmed past and began to move the baggage. Curtis stepped off the jetty and shook Marshall's hand.

"Better late than never I suppose but I do have four women to deal with," said Marshall with a smile.

"Five," put in the short brunette.

Curtis threw her a look and liked what he saw. She was just over five four and wore her curves in all the right places, black hair pulled back into a ponytail, olive skin and eyes that danced like lovers at midnight.

"Ah, how could I ever forget you Tammy."

"I'm not sure Will, how could you?"

Marshall grinned.

"Cap'n – may I introduce Miss Tammy Rodriguez."

"Captain," said Tammy shaking his hand.

"A pleasure."

She looked him in the eye and gave Curtis a smile.

"Likewise."

Marshall stepped in quickly.

"This is Tony Lewis, he's here to help me with the cameras."

The bearded man shook Don's hand.

"And this is Carmine Eco, the dresser for the models."

The short man reached in.

"Charmed. Oh, rough hands."

Curtis raised an eyebrow and then ushered them on board. The models went first and Marshall called them off to Don as they went.

"Heidi, Francesca, Nubia and Joelle."

Curtis nodded to each in turn. He watched as his crew stared at the women sashaying past and shook his head.

"Going to be one hell of a trip," he muttered to himself and then roared "get ready to cast off! Get that gear stowed away below. Chop-chop, we're already late – time to get moving."

3.

The sky was blue without a cloud, almost as blue as the sea that *The Ariadne* skipped across. Curtis smiled as he stood behind the wheel with a coffee cup in his hand. Samson lounged behind him sipping from his own cup.

"Good to be back out, eh?"

Curtis nodded glad to be away from the rotting harbour and the rotting people who infested it. He never felt as free as he did with *The Ariadne* beneath him and open sea to the front.

"Yeah, like nowhere else in the world."

"Reckon this'll just be a two night thing like you said?"

"How d'you mean?"

"You know these rich fuckers. Get there, see how beautiful it is, probably want to stay forever."

Curtis laughed.

"They keep pulling the money out and I'll stay."

"You got that straight, boss."

"Do me a favour and make sure the others are working and not staring at those model chicks."

"Roger that, Captain."

Samson headed out leaving Curtis alone with the helm.

*

William Marshall lay on the front on the converted crash boat in a pair of white Speedos, the models lay around him in wearing the latest pieces of fabric cut in various shapes but none much bigger than a slice of bacon. Carmine had a large portable cassette player, he pressed play and Freddie Mercury began singing about *Crazy Little Thing Called Love*.

"Time for bubbles, ladies? And maybe some blow – I think the sun is well and truly over the yard arm, or shall I check with Cap'n Curtis?"

Squeals and giggles greeted his announcement. Carmine was immediately on hand, in a pair of Speedos that were even smaller and tighter than Marshall's. He passed a glass vial of white powder to the photographer and another to Nubia.

"Oh, Tony," called Carmine.

Tony stuck his head around the wheelhouse where he had been taking pictures of his own of various parts of the boat.

"What?" Tony's London accent heavy was with annoyance.

"Be a darling and fetch us two bottles of the Bollinger."

Tony stared daggers at Carmine but went off to fetch the champagne.

"Fucking idiots aren't they?"

Curtis turned and saw Tammy Rodriguez leaning up against the doorframe of the wheelhouse. He looked out the window of the wheelhouse and watched them chopping and cutting lines of cocaine outside as Carmine popped the champagne.

"You don't like all that?"

"Not how they go on like it's the last days of Rome."

Curtis smiled.

"You drink though?"

"Yes."

"Want one?"

"A drink? Sure, as long as it isn't champagne."

Curtis tossed Tammy the keys to the gun cupboard.

"Then get the rum. I'll have one too."

Tammy splashed rum into two metal mugs and passed one over to Curtis.

"Cheers," he said and she held out her mug to be clinked.

Curtis watched through the window as Heidi, the blonde, removed her bikini top and threw it at Tony. He topped up her glass, put the bottle down and walked away back to his camera. The music changed from Queen to Blondie's *Heart of Glass*. Heidi poured champagne down her leg into Carmine's waiting mouth.

"What're you in this circus?" Curtis asked Tammy.

"I'm Marshall's assistant, which means I do everything from booking restaurants for him, managing his girlfriends and taking out his dry cleaning. Pretty much wipe his ass so he can take his pictures."

"Hope it pays well."

"Probably better than a boat captain in the middle of nowhere."

Curtis raised his mug.

"You got that right."

"So how come you're out here?"

"Because your boss paid me."

"No, I meant why are you up here doing this?"

"Well it's this or take out the occasional fishing trip, maybe deliver some cargo."

"But why?"

"Why not?" replied Curtis.

"What did you do back in Australia?"

"Not been back there in a while, worked on my Dad's fishing boat for a while. Six months after the war was enough for me."

"War?"

"Vietnam – you must know that one."

"Sure I know it, my brother died over there."

"Shit. I'm sorry."

Tammy shrugged.

"It is what it is."

She topped herself up and then Curtis. He took a sip and looked Tammy in the eye and she held his gaze. Shouting from outside pulled Curtis away. He set the wheel and stepped out.

"What the hell's going on out here?"

"That pervert is staring at me!" shouted Heidi.

Curtis looked at her for a moment and took in the white powder smeared around her nose and the erect nipples and wet legs, she really was something to stare at. He looked around to check exactly which pervert she meant. Gilbert, another of the local sailors and Samson's cousin, sat on top of the wheelhouse staring straight down at what Curtis saw with a lazy smile on his face.

"Nothing to do, Gil?"

"A few bits, Captain, but I kinda lost my track."

"Samson!"

Samson appeared from the hold.

"Sort your cousin out or I will."

Curtis went back into the wheelhouse and his rum. Marshall pushed in a moment later.

"Is that all you're going to do?"

"What should I do? Keelhaul him because your friend wants to get her tits out?"

Marshall sipped from his champagne flute.

"Make sure it doesn't happen again."

"Already done. Samson will keep them in line."

Marshall sniffed up deeply and went back outside. Curtis threw back his rum and held out his cup to Tammy. She laughed and topped him up.

"Is he any good as a photographer?"

Tammy nodded.

"He's the best. He's an asshole but people will put up with a lot when you're the best."

Curtis raised an eyebrow but kept his opinions to himself.

*

Gilbert sat in the aft of the boat, away from the party beyond the wheelhouse, scrubbing the deck that was already clean. Samson had set him to the task in a bid to keep him out of trouble and he muttered darkly as he dipped the brush into the bucket of soapy water. A murmur of voices came up from a gap in a hatch that had been propped open. After checking no one was around, Gil got down on his belly and snaked over to peek through the gap in the hatch.

He watched as Marshall entered the small cabin, champagne bottle in hand, and sat down on a bottom bunk. Gil continued to watch as Francesca followed Marshall into the cabin and knelt before him like a supplicant at an altar. She reached up and yanked Marshall's Speedos down, letting them pool around his ankles as she took his cock in her mouth. Gil grew hard as he watched Francesca's head bobbing in time with the swell of the ocean beneath the boat.

The door opened again and Heidi, the blonde woman, walked in still as naked as before except for her bikini bottoms. She stepped behind Francesca and ran her fingers through the dark haired model's tresses. Taking a tight grip she pushed the other woman's head down forcing her to take Marshall's cock deeper into her throat; Francesca gagged, Marshall moaned and Heidi laughed before leaning in to kiss Marshall. Gilbert continued to watch and slid a hand into his shorts letting his fingertips brush across the hard heat of his engorged cock.

"Gil, where are you?"

"Ah, shit," Gilbert whispered rolling away from the unfolding scene.

He went back to scrubbing the deck as Samson appeared from around the wheelhouse.

"Not finished yet?"

"Nearly – got a bit distracted."

Samson shook his head and walked away leaving Gilbert to his work and the thoughts which burned in his mind.

4.

The island came into sight as the sun began to duck lower on the horizon. Curtis looked out at it; golden sand on the beach, rich green jungle and rising to a black rocky high, a remnant of the islands volcanic past. So much space, around the island and beyond it, that it was the blue that drew the eye rather than the colours of the island – a dot in the forever.

Curtis took them in as close as he cared to and then shouted for Gilbert and Benjamin to drop the anchor. He sent Christopher and Samson to take the small boat and start shipping the supplies to the beach.

Marshall appeared from below decks in a short silk kimono, cigarette in one hand and a champagne flute in the other.

"Everything going okay, Captain?"

"Give us an hour and we'll have the tents set up and everything ready for you to go ashore."

Marshall nodded, threw his white-white smile and then vanished back below where the models were also resting.

*

They are here. I can see them. It has been so long since I have seen my enemies this close. I watch their ship and the smaller boat they send ashore with munitions. I give thanks to the Emperor for this opportunity to try and regain my honour which lies stained in the sticky dirt of this jungle hell.

Try to remember who I am and why I am here. It has been so long. So long since I have heard my own name. I whisper it to myself so that I will not forget. My name is Takahashi Ichiro and I serve the Emperor.

I check my own weapons; the sword of my ancestors, the ammunition, which I do not trust, for my rifle and the grenades which I do. But I have other weapons apart from these; weapons it has taken years for me to make and perfect.

It has been too many years that I have waited, I have been lax in my duty to let them come onto my island. Perhaps I should have attacked them as they came ashore. I watch. One man on the beach guarding the munitions. The boat goes back and returns with more boxes and leaves another man. They begin to pitch tents and I realise that they are coming for me. They are establishing their base camp – how many must I kill? I will kill them all for you. It has been too long since I have seen you and I love you more than my Emperor but not more than my duty.

I watch them come ashore and I know that not one of them will leave my island – they are but shades walking towards the veil. This is my island, my land, and they will be sore pressed to take it from me. I know why they are here and I will stop them.

*

Gilbert was staring back at the boat from the beach. Samson rapped him over the arm.

"What you doing?"

"Nothing. I'm allowed to fucking look."

"Not with your track record you're not."

Gilbert looked away.

"You know all that's finished. It was just a mistake."

"Mistake that nearly got you locked up or worse if that girl's dad had got hold of you. You stow that shit or I'll cut your balls off myself."

"Ah, cuz come on – you seen 'em, you can't blame me can you?"

Samson laughed.

"Yeah, suppose you're right. But any more of that pussy fever shit and I'll get the Captain to lock you in the hold."

Gilbert grinned.

"Nah, you're my cousin you wouldn't do that."

Samson wagged a finger in his face.

"Don't push your luck, Gil."

They went back to setting up the tents on the edge of the beach about ten yards from the treeline. Four tents went up and Benjamin, another local sailor, went off to find some firewood. He picked up a machete before heading into the closing dusk.

"What's the matter, Benjy, scared of the dark?" shouted Gilbert.

"Fuck off, Gil," came the response and Gilbert grinned.

"What about you, Chris?"

Christopher, looked at him.

"No, I ain't scared of the dark."

Gilbert laughed and risked a quick look to check that Samson was still checking the guide ropes of the tents.

"Nah, the girls – you like 'em?"

Christopher nodded.

"Good! Yeah, reckon we'll get some on this trip," said Gilbert.

He looked back out at *The Ariadne* and licked his lips.

5.

Tammy watched Curtis as he moved nimbly across the bow of the boat. She let her eyes move over his tall, lithe form. She found herself liking the Captain. How old was he? She wondered, older than her twenty six of that she was sure. He made her think of her brother when he had come home on leave, before he went on the tour from which he didn't return, something in his eyes. Curtis looked up, pushed his blonde hair off his brow and caught her look. He gave her an easy smile and she blushed and looked away.

Marshall, Carmine and the models had emerged from below decks, dressed now and ready to head over to the island. Tony Lewis stood with a camera, snapping a few shots as the sun slid away below the horizon colouring the few clouds red.

"Red sky at night, shepherd's delight," muttered Tony.

"What's that?" asked Marshall

"Nothing," replied Tony "just something that my mother used to say. Means that we're going to have a good day for it tomorrow."

"We've got a night to get through yet," said Marshall, slapping him on the arm with a smile and heading over to Don. "We set to get over there yet, Cap'n?"

Curtis nodded and pointed out to the darkening sea – the small boat was coming back towards them.

"I'll come over to the island with you and keep one crewman with me, the rest can sleep on the boat."

As Samson tied up the dinghy and clambered aboard, Don went and retrieved his rucksack and the M1 carbine from the gun safe. He checked the ammo pouch that was strapped to the stock; two fifteen round clips and another already loaded in the carbine. The remains of the bottle of rum went into his rucksack and he strapped his waterproof sleeping bag to the top.

"Samson."

Samson looked up.

"Boss?"

"I'm going to stay on the island with them tonight. I'll keep Benjy with me and the other two can bring the dinghy back and stay with you here on *Ariadne*."

Samson nodded and Curtis passed him the key to the gun locker.

"I'm taking the carbine but I left you the revolver just in case."

"In case what?"

Curtis laughed.

"Just in case!"

"Fair enough, boss."

A box of champagne and another of whiskey had been loaded into the dinghy along with food and lanterns.

"So who's coming on the first run?" asked Don.

Tammy stepped forward along with Nubia, Tony and Heidi. He helped them into the boat and then set himself to the oars. Don was happy to throw himself into something physical and he pulled at the oars, throwing the little boat towards the shore. They were soon on the beach and the boat was emptied.

"Christopher, Gilbert."

The two men approached.

"You two are staying on the ship with Samson tonight."

"Ah, what?"

Curtis put a finger up into Gilbert's face.

"Don't. You go back over with Christopher and he'll bring the others over. You stay with Samson."

Gilbert muttered under his breath as he helped Christopher push the dinghy back out into the surf and set off back towards *The Ariadne*. Benjy walked back from where he'd just got the fire going.

"Am I staying here with you, Mr Curtis?"

"Yeah, we'll split the watches. Probably not needed but…"

"Okay, want me to get the grub on?"

Curtis nodded.

"Please, Benjy, thanks – better get something into their stomachs before they crack those two crates open."

When Don looked away from the sea, at the darkening jungle that surrounded him, he was pulled back more than a decade to Phuoc Toy province in Vietnam. His hands tightened around the M1 as he scanned the dark. He thought of nights on picket, patrols through the shadowed halls beneath the trees hunting for a foe that seemed to dance away from them like ghosts. He thought of ambushes, booby traps and fire fights and of distant artillery falling like the wrath of a vengeful god.

"Penny for 'em?"

He turned and looked at Tammy who stood close by.

"Just thinking on the past, how a lot of places look the same."

Tammy reached out a hand and squeezed his shoulder. Curtis looked at her and gave her a weak smile. She tried to change the subject to pull him out of his maudlin mood.

"Tell me about the island."

"Not much to tell. To me it's just a name on a chart. Think there used to be a fishing village on the other side, uninhabited now."

"Why?"

Curtis shrugged.

"Maybe Samson knows. Not much here now – except us."

The fire blazed bright. Curtis turned and looked at Tammy.

"Do you take pictures?"

"No."

"Write or draw?"

She laughed.

"No, why?"

"Swim?"

"Yes," she looked at him, puzzled now.

Curtis nodded.

"Then let's go for a swim."

"Now?"

"Right now."

Curtis pulled off his shirt and lay it down on the sand, put the M1 down on top of it and kicked off his canvas deck shoes. After a moment Tammy shrugged and then smiled before pulling her shirt off and throwing it down on top of Curtis'. She wore a bikini top and left her shorts on. Curtis admired her body for a moment. Tammy saw him looking and smiled. She stepped out of her sandals and gestured at the sea.

"Oh, ladies first – I insist. Benjy! Watch the gun."

Benjamin looked over and shouted back.

"Why? What's it gonna do – a back flip?"

Tammy took off across the sand towards the ocean, kicking up sand, and Curtis followed racing her towards the surf. They hit the water in the same instant. It was still warm from the sun's kiss but the all-enveloping wetness of it still snatched their breath. Curtis rolled in the water and covered himself. He watched as Tammy turned and swam out further and the water made her hair turn inky black in the dusk. He reached for her but she wriggled away and swam out further, once again Curtis followed. When they were out far enough that their feet couldn't reach the bottom she spun and swam back close to him. They stared at each other in the darkness and below the water their hands moved over each other's bodies. Their mouths met and Tammy's legs locked around Curtis pulling them both down. They came back up coughing and laughing and swam back towards the beach.

When Curtis pulled himself out of the shallows he saw Marshall stood watching them.

"Mr Marshall."

Curtis ducked and picked up his shirt, slinging it over his shoulder before grabbing up the gun which he held by the sling.

"You should be careful, Cap'n."

"Why don't you just call me Don? That or else Captain Curtis."

Marshall smiled that smile of his, even whiter in the moonlight.

"Be careful of her, she'll have your soul."

Curtis stared back at him and then collected Tammy's clothes and turned to meet her as she emerged from the sea.

*

I watch them and think of you my love. The Gaijin frolics in the sea with the woman while others move around. The tents are ready now and they have brought more comfort wives than I think necessary. It matters little. They will all be dead soon. I watch the boat and realise that it must go first. Even in the dead light I see three shapes moving on it. They are ghosts, that is all they are. The people of the beach are ghosts as the villagers who dwelt here before them were ghosts. They are not real to me, not part of my world. They are already dead but they do not know it yet. They soon will.

6.

They drank into the night, champagne and whiskey and finished the glass vials, snorting the powder greedily. In the firelight they danced to the disco music that played on Carmine's tape deck. Curtis watched them from the edge of camp. Benjy approached.

"Think they want you to join them, boss."

Curtis shrugged.

"The day when I'd rather drink with rich pricks than walk the watch ain't here yet,"

Benjy coughed and pointed towards Tammy and Tony who sat away from the rest.

"Let me take the watch."

Curtis thought for a moment and then passed the M1 to Benjy.

"Cheers."

"No problem, boss you can take over from me at four."

Benjy dropped him a wink and Curtis walked over to Tammy and Tony. Tammy smiled and passed him a cup of whiskey. Tony gave him a nod and he sat down cross-legged with them.

Tammy leaned in and shared her warmth. Tony filled a mug with whiskey and passed it to Curtis. He took a sip and let the whiskey burn down into his gut.

"It's good stuff."

Tony nodded.

"Only the best for, *Mister* Marshall."

He raised an eyebrow at Curtis and took a healthy tug on his own drink. Curtis laughed and lit a cigarette.

"How in the hell did you end up with him?"

Tony shrugged.

"Jobs a job and this way I get to see the world."

"You take pics yourself though?"

"Yes, not for quite the same amounts that get paid for his."

"Still, they're yours."

Tony nodded and smiled

"Exactly."

*

The Ariadne swayed with the tide and Samson watched Gilbert press his nose against the glass to look at the beach.

"Stop that shit, Gil."

"Ain't doing nothing."

Samson made to come out of his chair and Gilbert backed away from the window.

"I may as well go to bed than put up with this – fuckin' torture."

"Go to bed then."

Gilbert threw a look at his cousin and stomped out of the wheelhouse. With a sigh Samson looked out at the fire on the beach and then at Christopher who sat in the corner.

"You want a drink?"

Christopher nodded and Samson pulled out Don's second bottle that he kept stashed underneath the captain's chair. They shared a couple of snifters and then a couple more knowing that the Captain wouldn't begrudge them a drink or three as long as the boat was looked after and a watch maintained.

*

Samson awoke suddenly. He looked around the wheelhouse and saw Christopher curled up in his corner seat. Samson got up and rubbed the sleep from his eyes. He checked the time and saw it was just before five. Swinging himself out of his seat, Samson walked out unsteadily to the deck. He found his cigarettes and lit one, stopping to watch as the rising sun began to colour the sky. When the cigarette was done he flicked it overboard and turned to go back into the wheelhouse – thinking of a pot of coffee and a slow wake up, when he stopped. He turned back and saw the wet footprints on the deck. Samson looked around but saw nothing and no one. He walked over to the door which led down to the quarters, opened it and shouted down.

"Gilbert! Gil, get up, mate."

There was no answer. Samson climbed down and checked that no one was there. Stupid bastard, he thought, Curtis would have his fucking hide if he'd swum over to the island to see the women. Then a thought struck Samson – if Gilbert had swum over to the island then why were there wet footprints on the deck if he hadn't come back? Samson's gut tightened and he headed back to the wheelhouse fumbling for the key that Don had given him. Inside he shook Christopher awake and unlocked the gun cupboard. The long-barrelled, black .357 looked at him and he grabbed at it, checked the load and then looked to Christopher.

"Might be there's someone on the boat."

"Like who?"

"If I knew that I wouldn't need the bloody gun," replied Samson as he strapped on the gun belt and holster for the pistol.

Christopher nodded and drew the lock knife from his belt. He nodded once to Samson and they moved off to search the boat.

*

The need to piss pulled Heidi out of her sleep. She climbed out from beneath her thin sheet and stepped over Nubia to reach the flap of the tent. The sky had begun to lighten as she emerged and crossed the sand looking for somewhere private. She moved into the tree line and pushed on until she was well out of eyeshot of the camp. Finally she crouched down and pulled down her panties. She sighed as she relieved her champagne-strained bladder.

"Even when you piss you look good."

Heidi tried to turn and ended up falling back into her own puddle. Gilbert sat, crouched, on a fallen log to her left. He was only wearing a pair of small shorts, still wet from his swim over and in his hand he held a short bladed knife.

"Shit, even sitting in your own piss you look good."

Gilbert hopped down from the log.

"I saw how you were looking at me earlier."

Heidi shook her head.

"I wasn't."

"Yeah, you were. Just me and you now so no need to make shit up."

Scooting back Heidi looked around but the line of trees blocked her sight of camp. She prepared to scream as Gilbert stepped closer.

*

They checked the deck quickly, Samson with the revolver outstretched and Christopher hanging back with his knife. Samson stopped.

"I want the boss over here, this isn't right."

He grabbed up a torch and headed to the starboard side to try and signal Don. Christopher turned and looked at the door to the engine room.

"Samson, we haven't checked down here."

"Leave it."

Even as Samson spoke Christopher tugged apart the doors to the engine room. As the doors opened a wire slid sideways and pulled the pin from the grenade. In the second before it went off Christopher stared at the olive green shell and the brass head. It popped with a flash of light and Samson threw up his arm, feeling the burn of shrapnel cutting into the muscles of the limb as he did. Christopher screamed and Samson tried to scramble across the deck to him. Boom-boom went two more explosions that rocked *The Ariadne*. Samson was thrown sideways and hit the rail. He turned to see Christopher walking towards him extending handless arms that dripped red.

*

With one hand undoing the flies of his shorts, Gilbert stepped toward the prone Heidi. She scrambled back and screamed. Gilbert's face twisted to anger.

"Now why did you want to do that? I know you want me."

"I don't fucking want you."

Heidi's foot kicked out and connected with the side of Gilbert's knee. He dropped and she scrambled to her feet and turned to run. Gilbert swung his knife towards her neck but was surprised when it seemed to halt in mid-air. He watched as his hand fell away, dirt catching on the bloody stump. Heidi turned and saw the rolling hand and screamed again.

"Fuck," said Gilbert trying to work out what had happened to his hand.

Regaining her feet Heidi turned and ran back towards the camp. Gilbert turned and, with the stump of his wrist pressed tight against himself, walked in the opposite direction with a stumbling gait, the life dripping out of him. After a few yards he heard the crunch of a branch underfoot and turned. There was nothing there. He turned back and the blade kissed his throat. In a single sweep Gilbert's head was separated from his shoulders and sent to bounce back across the clearing to come to a rest in the puddle of Heidi's piss.

*

If the screams from the woods didn't wake him up the explosion from his boat certainly did. Curtis snapped awake and saw a sleepy looking Benjy come running in fumbling with the M1. Curtis jumped out from his sleeping bag and grabbed the gun. He dropped to one knee and checked the weapon was ready to fire.

"I thought I'd let you sleep for a bit, boss."

"Grab a machete and get near the tents."

Benjy nodded and grabbed up a long knife. Curtis looked around, saw the pall of smoke rising from *The Ariadne* and was torn. He looked back and forth for a moment, swore, and then headed for the tree-line where the screams had come from. He kept the carbine tight into his shoulder as he ran, finger outside the trigger guard. Heidi stumbled from the bush and Curtis aimed the carbine straight at her blonde head. She stopped dead and looked straight at him. Curtis stared at her down the barrel for a moment and then pulled it up.

"Who's in there?"

Heidi's mouth moved but no sound came out. Curtis looked at her for a moment and then pushed past her into the trees. He moved slowly, picking his positions and stopping to listen as he went, the carbine tight to his shoulder. Curtis found Gilbert's severed hand and head first. He looked at them for a moment and then moved up to the rest of his body. He dropped to one knee and scanned the jungle. Noise filled his ears; clicking insects, the screech of birds, shouts from the camp. Curtis stood and worked his way back to the beach keeping the M1 pointed at the jungle as he did.

The camp was up and moving when Curtis got back. Marshall was walking around in his Speedos with a small silver pistol in his hand, a Walther PPK – James Bond's gun. He brought his hand up as the Captain came out of the tree-line. Curtis gave him a moment and was glad when the American let the pistol drop.

"What the fuck is going on here, Curtis?"

Curtis shrugged.

"Someone's took Gilbert's head off and fuck knows what's happened to my boat. I'll give you a clue Mr Marshall – step the fuck off me and let me find out what's going on."

Marshall made to raise the pistol but Curtis grabbed his wrist and stared straight into his eyes.

"Get in my way, Mr Marshall and I will fuck you up. Keep the gun down and watch the tree-line for me."

For a moment Marshall looked like he would argue but he saw the look in Curtis' eyes and stepped away. He knelt down and pointed the Walther PPK he carried at the tree-line. Curtis nodded and moved off heading for the surf. Everyone had come out of the tents and Curtis felt their eyes on him as he hit the surf. He watched the boat as it came towards them from *The Ariadne*. When it got close Curtis dashed out and helped pull it up onto the beach. Christopher was pale and unmoving, Samson's right arm a mass of red torn flesh. Curtis helped get the two men out of the boat and onto the beach. Tammy had the medical kit open and was trying to get a bandage wrapped around his arm.

"What the fuck happened?" asked Curtis.

"Booby trap. Chris opened the hatch and it took his hands, there must've been something hooked up to the door and more below the surface. One in the engine and two for the deck. Engine's in bits and there's a hole in the hull."

"Who?" asked Curtis.

Samson shrugged.

"Didn't see a fuckin' thing. Flashed white and took the boy's hands off. There was wet footprints on the deck. There's someone else here on the island, boss."

Curtis looked at his injured crewman and then at his stricken boat.

"Shit," he said and turned away.

7.

They stood on the beach and watched *The Ariadne* go down. There were tears in Curtis' eyes but he pushed them away. Christopher lay covered by a blanket near the tents. They had brought Gilbert's body back and he lay likewise covered.

"An SOS, we need to send an SOS," said Marshall.

Curtis looked at him for a moment before he spoke.

"Samson would have done that before he got clear. But round here they aren't that quick. Could be tomorrow at least before they get to us."

"So we have to wait here on the beach?" asked Joelle.

Curtis nodded.

"We stay here and don't go near the trees."

Joelle threw a look at Heidi who sat alone, a throw around her shoulders. Carmine went over and sat next to her. He started talking and she stopped shaking and listened. Curtis and Tony carried Samson from the dinghy and put him down on the sand. The Captain stripped the pistol belt from him and offered it to Tony.

"Don't have a clue. I could put it on but I'd be next to useless."

Curtis walked over to Carmine.

"You know how to use this?"

"I might be a fruit but I'm an Italian from Brooklyn – of course I know how to use it. Give it here," he strapped the gun belt on and sighed "dirty green army surplus, not really my colour but it'll have to do."

Curtis went back to Samson and lifted his head.

"You did put out the distress call didn't you?"

"Wasn't time, boss."

Curtis looked up at the sky.

"So no one knows we're out here?"

Samson bit back a wave of pain from his ruined arm and nodded.

"Shit," said Curtis, "Marshall!"

Marshall walked over, pistol pointed at the sand and a bottle of Johnny Walker in his other hand.

"He didn't get a chance to get an SOS out."

Marshall looked blank.

"No one's coming for us."

"They'll have to. They will. I'm William Marshall."

Curtis stared at him and wondered when he'd realise that help wasn't coming but Marshall simply shook his head and took a hit off his bottle.

*

They are on my island forever now that I have taken their boat.

I came across two of the interlopers and took one's head –there are many more to come. I watch them moving around trying to secure the perimeter that I have already penetrated. I know how this game will play out. I have had the longest time to think about every movement that my opponents can make and I know them all. Let them try.

8.

Curtis was down on one knee thinking. Marshall had been pacing back and forth but now sat on the sand, the night's booze and cocaine catching up with him. He wore a Nikon around his neck like a giant medallion. He looked over at Curtis and then spoke.

"So what's the plan?"

"Plan?"

"I'm presuming you've got a plan."

Curtis shrugged.

"At the minute all I've got are some thoughts."

"Let's hear them," asked Joelle.

Curtis looked up at her and nodded.

"The way I see it if there's someone else on the island that means they've got a means to get off it - a boat, something. We can try and find it. Failing that we light a bloody big fire on top of the mountain and hope someone sees it."

The others had gathered around, except Samson who lay resting in one of the tents. There were nods of agreement.

"How long will the food last?" asked Carmine.

Curtis weighed it up.

"A couple of days if we're careful. We'll need to find some fresh water, look for fruit if we can."

"What about our *friend* out in the jungle?" asked Marshall.

Curtis shrugged.

"Not much we can do except keep watch. We've got three guns, not a lot of ammo but it'll have to do. We don't even know how many of them there are."

Benjy gripped his machete tighter and stared out at the green of the jungle. The others had begun to arm themselves; Curtis had the M1, Marshall and Carmine pistols, Nubia had picked up another machete and Joelle held a piece of firewood like a club.

"We have to do something," said Tammy.

Curtis nodded.

"Maybe we need to get out and look for the boat whoever is on the island is using."

"What about that?" asked Marshall.

Curtis turned and saw that he was pointing to the dinghy.

"What about it?"

"Could someone go for help?"

"Help? Man, it would take a week to get back – if you didn't get lost."

But the dinghy had set Curtis to thinking.

"We can use it though. If we put the supplies and a couple of people in it then the boat can follow us around the shoreline while we look for whoever's here. If we haven't found anything by nightfall then we camp on the beach and head for the high ground tomorrow to get a beacon lit."

There was no dissent to Curtis' suggestion so he nodded and looked around at the group.

"Tony, you and Francesca take Samson in the dinghy with the supplies and the rest of us will move along the shore."

Nods and they loaded up the dinghy. Samson tried to argue but he was pale and Curtis ordered him into the dinghy.

"Got to have one real sailor with the landlubbers, eh?"

Samson forced a weak smile.

"Alright, Captain, I'll try to keep them out of trouble."

*

With the dinghy out beyond the breaks, following them, Curtis took point and led the group off along the beach.

"Keep your eyes peeled, watch the trees and look out for signs of anyone being about – footprints, anything."

Out on the left Carmine walked and watched the jungle, he left the pistol in its holster but kept the flap unbuttoned. Marshall brought up the rear, gun in hand. Benjy padded up next to Curtis.

"Think we'll find anything, Captain?"

Curtis shrugged.

"Stands to reason there'll be a boat."

"I'm not worried about that, I'm worrying we'll find whoever did for Gil when we find their boat."

"Well there're enough of us."

Benjy looked back at the rest of the bunch.

"I hate to say it, Captain, but this lot look more likely to hurt themselves than anyone we come across."

"What's the alternative?"

"I could take the boat and go for help. Rather be on the open sea than here. Place is fuckin' cursed."

"Cursed?"

"Yeah. That's the way me grandmother told it."

"Cursed how?"

"Bad shit happened here. People always going missing. In the end the village just closed up and they all shipped off."

"The village, of course. You think they might have left any boats?"

"Be rotted to shit by now. Houses might still be there though."

"You know where it is?"

Benjy shook his head.

"Nah, but if we're walking the beach I reckon we'll run across it."

Curtis was about to nod when a shot rang out.

"Shit," Curtis ducked down to one knee and looked down the beach.

The rest of the group scattered, Joelle diving for the tall grass at the edge of the trees. Benjy ducked down next to the Captain. About two hundred yards down the beach was a pile of driftwood and other flotsam. Curtis watched the pile and saw the flash before he heard the second shot. Marshall stood in a crouched, two-handed shooting stance – the type they teach at expensive LA shooting ranges. He fired once and then again.

"Save your ammo," shouted Curtis as he sighted in his carbine. He took a breath and then let it out in a long stream.

"Go on, Captain. Get the bastard."

Curtis blanked out Benjy, the glare of the sun, the scream from the edge of the trees and the fact that there was someone shooting at him. A squeeze of the trigger and Curtis put a three round burst into the driftwood. Chunks of wood were blasted off. Curtis watched a figure rise and saw the rifle pointed down the beach straight at him. He waited for the shot but none came. The figure fumbled with the rifle and Curtis smiled.

"Stoppage!"

He lined up the M1 and snapped off a single shot. The figure ducked and ran for the trees. Curtis stood and fired another three round burst. The shots chased the figure into the trees but none struck home.

"Don!"

Curtis turned at Tammy's call and jogged over to where she stood. He wondered what she was looking at but then looked down and saw the shallow pit. Joelle lay in the pit, moaning in agony. The pit was lined with short, sharpened bamboo stakes and Joelle had leapt straight onto them as she dived for cover in the grass. Curtis ducked down and caught a whiff of shit. He looked closely at the stakes and saw that the tips were stained brown.

"Ah, Jesus."

Joelle moaned again.

"What do we do?" asked Tammy.

"You still got the medical kit?"

Tammy nodded.

"Well we have to get her off those stakes but when we do she's going to bleed like a stuck pig. When we get her up you put every bit of antiseptic in that kit on her wounds. Benjy!"

"Captain?"

"You take this," he passed him the M1 "and watch the trees in case he comes back. Carmine, Marshall – you'll have to help me."

Carmine stepped up and looked into the pit. He shook his head and then holstered the .357. Marshall stayed back.

"I can't."

"C'mon, man. She needs you."

Marshall shook his head.

"I don't want to see her like that. I want to remember her the way she was."

"She's still alive you prick! Get over here and help us or I swear to God I'll kill you long before our friend in the jungle."

Marshall stared death at Curtis but then put the safety on the Walther and pushed it into the pocket of his shorts. The three men stared down at the girl in the pit and then set to work trying to pull her up and off the stakes. She screamed as they lifted her and when they laid her down she stained the grass red. Curtis was surprised that the stakes hadn't managed to sever anything vital. The sharpened bamboo had stabbed into her flesh in, perhaps, nine or ten places like shallow knife wounds. Tammy moved in with what remained of the bandages, but it wasn't the bleeding that worried Curtis – it was the filth that had coated the stakes. Curtis looked out to sea but the dinghy was nowhere to be seen. He looked around watched as Marshall snapped a couple of shots of the pit with his Nikon.

"What are you doing?"

Marshall shrugged and pointed the camera at Curtis.

"Want me to take yours instead."

Curtis stared at him until he lowered the camera.

9.

Under the shaded canopy of trees Tony struggled with the oars of the boat. He swore and tried to dig the oars into the water but the dinghy seemed to be pushed further into the shadowy jungle. They had heard the shots on the beach but try as he might Tony could not slow the dinghy and it had sped past the sniper. When he had tried to turn into the shore they had ended up on a small river that took them inland. Francesca looked at Tony, eyes big, and Samson tried to pull himself up.

"Get in to the bank."

Tony nodded and tried.

"I'm not very good with these."

"Fuck, man."

Samson pushed him away and took over at the oars. He pulled and turned the dinghy towards the bank, fresh red blossoming on the white of his bandaged arm. They came to a stop and they all sat in silence – the jungle shadowy and vast around them, birds called out and insects crawled.

"Shit. We haven't got a gun," muttered Samson.

Tony listened to the sounds of the forest and looked around.

"You don't think he's anywhere around here do you?"

Francesca shook her head.

"We must have moved well past him."

Samson managed to pull the knife from his belt and climbed out onto the bank.

"We need to get the Captain and the others."

"I don't want to go out there. Why don't we paddle back out to the sea?"

"You could be right," replied Samson.

Before Samson could climb back into the boat he felt something behind him and half-turned as the bayonet bit through his spine. The big sailor screamed and dropped into the dirt, the feeling in his legs already a vague memory. The man who stood behind him was short and Asian, skin kissed dark by the sun, with hair that was greying and receding. He wore a jacket that had once been green but was now a washed-out, weather beaten, grey. Francesca screamed and the man smiled. On the ground Samson flapped around like a landed fish and tried to swing his blade up at the man's groin. He beat the blade away with his bayoneted rifle and speared

Samson's wrist to the ground. The big man screamed and tried to buck away from the fresh pain. With a twist and a turn the bayonet was removed and the man held it poised for a moment before stabbing it down through Samson's eye, slicing through brain and skull with a wet crunch.

Francesca leapt from the dinghy and crashed into the water. It was shallow and she began to wade away towards the opposite bank. The man withdrew the bayonet from Samson's head and raised the rifle. He slid back the bolt slowly and deliberately and Francesca froze. Tony sat with his hands held up.

"Franny, stop," and then turning back to the man on the bank "let's just talk about this."

The man looked at Tony and the photo technician continued to talk.

"Is that a Japanese army jacket? I know it is. I've seen them before when I was in Tokyo. You've been here since the war? It's over you know, the war? Over a long time now the last of you guys walked out of the jungle a couple of years ago."

The man continued to watch Tony and listen.

"We're not here to try and harm you. Just here for pictures. Please, can you understand me? Do you speak English?"

Francesca stood in the shallows, frozen in place, watching the exchange between the two men. They watched as the man lay down his rifle on the bank. Tony smiled.

"Thank you. That's it, let's be calm and talk. Let's just talk some more."

Tony half stood in the dinghy. The man turned away.

"Wait..." said Tony.

The man turned, drawing the katana as he came. The blade rose high above them and Tony had a moment to admire the unblemished steel before it descended in an arc towards him.

"No!"

The blade took him through the top of his head and cut down, bone and flesh butter beneath the sword, until in hit Tony's pelvic bone. The two halves of him began to peel away from each other like a split banana. Tony was no longer able to scream but Francesca screamed for both of them. The man withdrew the blade and hacked Tony off at the knees, bone and sinew giving little resistance to the razor sharp folded steel. After Tony fell the man looked down at Francesca for a moment and then marched down into the river to get her.

10.

Joelle had lost consciousness not long after Tammy had finished bandaging her up. She lay on the sand with the other women crowded around her. Joelle's golden skin had lost its colour and she was as grey as gruel. She murmured in fevered dream.

"We need to get her to help."

Heidi looked at Nubia and nodded.

"How in the hell are we going to do that?" threw in Marshall from where he sat.

Curtis and Benjy were hacking down branches from the trees at the edge of the jungle while Carmine kept watch. Tammy broke away from the others and approached Curtis.

"What are we going to do, Don?"

Curtis gestured at the branches.

"Going to try and rig up a stretcher for her. Then we head for the higher ground, try to reach the peak by nightfall and get a fire lit."

"What about the dinghy?"

Curtis shrugged.

"They must've been caught by the tide. Samson should get them turned around. They'll be back."

"What if they're not?"

"Then I'll have to go and look for them. How is she?"

"Not good. She lost a lot of blood."

"She'll survive that but if those wounds get infected the shock could kill her."

"What kind of person makes something like that pit?"

Curtis looked away.

"Saw ones like it in Vietnam. I think people have been coming up with ways to hurt each other since the Garden of Eden, this isn't anything new."

They used large leaves and a couple of rain ponchos to make up the body of the stretcher, lashing them to the branches they had cut. Carmine walked back.

"Not seeing anything out there, Captain."

"Well he's out there somewhere. I'm just glad his rifle jammed up when it did."

Marshall finally got up from the sand.

"So we'll drag her on that?" he gestured at the stretcher and Curtis nodded.

They gathered up their kit and got Joelle moved onto the stretcher. Curtis looked out to sea but saw nothing of the dinghy. He sighed

"Benjy, you reckon you can lead them towards the mountain?"

"Yes, Captain."

"Guess I'll have to go and look for them."

"Leave them, they'll catch up," said Marshall.

"I can't do that, Mr Marshall. Samson's hurt and they haven't got a gun with them. They'll need help and to be told we're heading up the mountain."

"You're taking your gun?"

"Of course."

Marshall nodded.

"Then I guess we'd better hope the pistols keep us safe."

"I'll catch you up as soon as I can."

Tammy walked over.

"Want me to come with you, Don?"

Curtis smiled.

"Best you stay with the others. I can move faster alone."

She nodded and reached out to squeeze his hand.

"Be careful."

"Always," he replied.

11.

Beneath the dark canopy Francesca stumbled along a path that was about a foot wide. A length of twine was tied around her throat and was held by the man like he was walking a Poodle in the park. The katana was back in its scabbard and he had the rifle slung over his shoulder. Francesca's foot slipped on a mossy rock and she stumbled. Feeling the lead slacken she threw herself off to the side of the path and yanked the twine from the man's hand. She plunged into the bushes and began to run. Branches lashed at her flesh as she ran down the slope. The ground grew steeper and rocks lurked beneath the shrubbery. One of the rocks caught her toe and spilled her over. She hit the ground hard and rolled further down until she felt nothing but air beneath her.

Francesca fell ten feet or so and landed heavily on rocks which lay below. The pain was instant and burned white-hot through her. She screamed instinctively. She looked down and saw her knee twisted at an unnatural angle. She screamed again and continued to until the man appeared above her. He stared down at her for a moment and then climbed down the rocks with the dexterity of a mountain goat. He stood over her. No point taking her further but she could still be of use.

*

Down in the jungle Curtis heard the screams. He moved carefully forward watching for any surprises that might have been left for him. In his mind he wasn't sure whether he was on the island or back in the jungles of Phuoc Toy but then it didn't matter, not really. All that mattered was to play the game – stay alive no matter what the cost. Curtis swapped out the half-empty clip from the M1 and replaced it with a full one. He had no tape to try and fashion a jungle clip like they had back in Vietnam. Thirty eight rounds left but the Captain knew that that was nothing, it could be gone in a three minute fire-fight.

He came across the river and saw the deflated dinghy floating in it. A long slash ran along the side of the little boat. Checking the slash Curtis could see that it looked too clean to be caused by the boat getting caught up on rocks. He brought the carbine up to his shoulder and moved forward carefully. He followed the river back towards the sea and soon came across what he had hoped not to find; a pair of corpses. He looked at what remained of Tony in the shallows. Looking away from the split open cadaver he checked Samson, saw his one whole eye glassy and staring up at the canopy.

"Shit!"

Curtis looked around. He could feel the rage rising but knew that the emotion was useless to him and pushed it away. He would kill the man who had done this, like he had killed men before. Looking down at his dead friend he vowed it and then tried to make sense of the mess of footprints. He could see the tracks leading down into the shallows of the river and guessed that Francesca had been in the water. Checking both banks he found no other footprints. He looked at the river and smiled.

"Clever little fucker, aren't you."

He stepped into the river and began to walk upstream his own tracks as hidden by the water as those of the man he pursued.

*

The main body of the group was moving slowly. Benjy was leading them while Tammy and Carmine dragged the stretcher. Nubia and Heidi moved on the flanks, watching the bushes, and Marshall brought up the rear. There was no track to speak of but Benjy tried to keep them moving where the brush was at its thinnest. Marshall changed his grip on the Walther and moved past the stretcher so that he was level with Benjy.

"How much further?"

The young sailor looked at the photographer.

"Hours yet, boss."

"We'll have to rest. They can't carry her much longer."

Benjy looked around before nodding.

"Okay. Let's take a break."

Marshall smiled and gestured at the others to take a rest. He pulled a pack of cigarettes from his pocket and offered them to Benjy who took one happily. Marshall lit him with his silver Ronson.

"You think the Captain will be back?"

Benjy grinned.

"Course he will. Shit, you don't know Captain Curtis."

"No?"

"Nah, fella from over in Port Robinson tried to get him once."

"Get him?"

"Reckoned the Captain had nicked one of his jobs, lying bastard. Anyway he came looking and caught the Captain on his own. Bastard had two mates with him and they all had knives."

Benjy paused and took a deep toke on his cigarette.

"And?"

"And? Captain Curtis fucked them up. Before he came up here he was army, saw some bad shit. Cool head like you don't see on many men. Nah, my money's on the Captain – he'll be back."

Marshall nodded and filed the words away. He looked around and saw the others still sitting. Carmine held his canteen to his mouth but then moved it away and upended it. A single drop fell from it.

"Going to need water soon."

Benjy looked around.

"We'll keep on for the mountain. Probably run across a spring or something on the way."

After a few minutes they climbed to their feet and pushed on into the green hell. Benjy held on tightly to his machete, occasionally swinging it to clear some stubborn vines or bush. When they had been walking for another quarter of an hour Benjy stopped. He thought that he could hear something in the jungle ahead. He held up his hand to stop the group. Leaning forward he strained to hear and discern the sound. Unable to work out what the sound was Benjy put his hand up again and gestured for them to keep moving. A few minutes later they stepped into a clearing and Benjy saw the source of the sound; Francesca was hanging upside down from a tree, her feet tied to it with vines, she was a mass of red and it looked as though she had simply burst out of her own skin. Benjy looked closer and could see that her skin had been sliced away until all that remained was the red mass of exposed tissue. Flies buzzed around the hanging form.

"Jesus!" he looked away.

Marshall stared. He took in the blood, the hacked flesh and the gag in her mouth. But worse than the sight was the sound. Even through the gag they could hear her, mewling like a dying animal that needed to be put out of its misery.

"Cut her down," muttered Marshall.

Benjy forced himself to look at the hanging woman and then moved towards her with his machete. He reached past her ruined flesh and grabbed at the vines. He saw the wire a moment after he should have. The wire pulled the pin from the grenade that had been pushed deep between the cheeks of Francesca's arse. Benjy looked at the brass head of the grenade sticking out of her and he sighed.

"Fuck sake."

The grenade went off and as well as blowing Francesca apart the shrapnel punched into Benjy's head and hurled him to the floor. Marshall stumbled back. He was covered in pieces of Francesca. He held the gun up and pointed it out into the trees all the while trying to compute exactly what had gone wrong in his life that had put him in the place he now found himself. But even in that moment as the shock rescinded Marshall looked towards what was left of Francesca. He lowered the Walther and raised the lens of his camera.

12.

The low thump of an explosion from somewhere off to his left made Curtis' ears prick up. He stopped and listened. The noise had sent a flock of birds racing up into the blue sky. Curtis waited but heard nothing further except for the sounds of the jungle. He moved to the riverbank and snatched a quick drink from his canteen before pushing on. A minute or two later he found where they had left the river. The tracks showed bare feet followed by bare feet, both sets small.

Curtis followed the tracks, nothing on his mind but moving forward carefully and closing in on the man who had already caused so much destruction. He watched for wires and freshly moved earth as he stepped through the undergrowth. Curtis found himself whispering to a God he had not tried to speak to in a long time and he hoped for an answer this time; an answer or a sign, anything, to show that he was doing the right thing. But as before, when he had whispered into the void after he watched friends die, there was nothing.

*

They are nothing, mere cattle before a wolf. I kill them as I choose and already I have reduced their numbers by six. I can smell the death on the seventh, the one they drag with them. Their path is obvious – they are headed for the high ground. Headed for my mountain. They will die before they reach the peak. It is my duty that they do not get further and I will always do my duty.

*

After he wiped the sick away from his mouth Marshall looked at what was left of his little band; Heidi, Nubia, Carmine, Tammy and Joelle unconscious on the stretcher.

"What do we do, Will?" asked Carmine.

Marshall shrugged.

"Where the fuck is Curtis?"

"He won't be back," said Heidi.

Tammy threw her a look.

"Yes, he will. He'll be back with the others."

"The others are dead too," snapped the blonde woman "all dead. Just like we're going to be if we don't fucking do something."

Marshall looked up.

"Oh no. No. I'm not dying here," he looked up at the mountain, "we stick with the plan and push for the top. Get a beacon lit and wait for help. Once we have the high ground we'll have an advantage. Carmine, you help me and we'll pull the stretcher double time."

Carmine nodded and stripped off his gun belt.

"Any of you dolls know how to use this?"

Nubia and Tammy shook their heads but Heidi stepped forward and took the pistol, strapping it on to her waist.

"I did some shooting growing up in the Tyrol. It has been a long time but if that bastard comes at us I will get him."

"Alright, Heidi She-Wolf, I like that fighting-talk."

Carmine pushed his sunglasses back up his nose and picked up his side of the stretcher. Tammy looked at Marshall.

"Want me to take the other gun? I'm not great but I know which end is which."

"No. I'll keep it."

She stared at him but he ignored her and reached down to the stretcher.

"Let's go."

They moved past what was left of Francesca and Benjy, averting their eyes and concentrating on putting one foot in front of the other. They started off fast but the stretcher and the woman on it were heavier than they looked and they soon slowed. All the time they pushed on they checked the dark places between the trees and bushes scared for what might emerge or be waiting for them.

Marshall held up a hand and they paused.

"This is crazy. We can't make it up there by night carrying her."

Tammy stepped forward.

"What the fuck are you suggesting, Will?"

The photographer shrugged and took the pistol from his pocket.

"She doesn't look so good, looks like she won't make it anyway."

"I'll ask again, Will – what the fuck are you saying?"

"Just that the way I see it we have two options."

"And they are?"

"Either someone waits here with her and the rest of us push on to get the beacon lit or…"

"Or? Just say exactly what it is you're thinking," Tammy's hands clenched into fists.

"Well it would be kinder."

Nubia looked at Marshall.

"No, Will, that's…"

"What? What is it? It's what'll keep the rest of us alive is what it is."

Tammy looked to Heidi and the only other gun.

"Will is right."

Tammy swore and stamped her foot.

"I won't let you."

Heidi drew the .357. She didn't point it anywhere but the threat was there.

"Carmine?" implored Tammy.

The little dresser shook his head.

"It isn't right, Will."

"That's three against two, Will. Put the idea out of your head and pick up the stretcher."

There was a half-smile on Marshall's face. The pistol was held loosely in his hand but the report of it made everyone jump. The bullet had hit Joelle in the chest, she hadn't made a sound, had simply given up holding on.

"Fuck three against two. The guns make the law here. I just saved all your lives."

Marshall turned and pushed on towards the mountain. Heidi followed, revolver still in her hand. Nubia waited a moment and then went after them.

"Carmine?" asked Tammy.

He shrugged at her.

"It's fucked up but we have to stick together."

Tammy shook her head.

"He'll do the same to you if you slow him down."

"I don't intend to give him an excuse - or a chance if it comes to it."

Carmine turned and ran after the others leaving Tammy with Joelle's corpse. Tammy stared down at the dead woman and then turned and watched Carmine disappear after the others.

13.

Curtis followed the shape of a man moving in the shadows of the trees down in a gully a hundred yards in front of him. He paused and wiped the sweat from his eyes before lifting the carbine and tracking the shape once again. The figure paused and looked around as though he could feel eyes on him. Curtis fired. A tight three round burst followed by a second. The shade dropped but then came up again and ran. Curtis rose from one knee and tracked the movement before he squeezed the trigger again, sending another three rounds into the trees.

Using roots and rocks as hand and foot holds Curtis descended into the gully and then tracked towards where he had sighted the figure. He did not rush. He moved with the same slow deliberation that had got him into position above their attacker. It took the better part of twenty minutes to get to the spot where he had seen the figure. Curtis watched the trees as he stepped carefully. He found the rifle with the bayonet still attached. He checked the weapon quickly and could see it was jammed but he took no chances and stripped the bolt from the weapon, putting the essential piece of the mechanism into his pocket. Further on there was blood on the ground, not a lot but some. Curtis knew he had at least clipped the man, maybe more. He was human at least, he could bleed therefore he could die.

*

Shots sounded out in the jungle and Tammy's head snapped up. She took a look at Joelle's body on the stretcher and then moved quickly into the bushes. The shots had been close and Tammy felt fear rise up in her, the fingers of terror teasing and caressing her stomach. She looked around and found a piece of wood that looked like it was of a decent enough weight to lay a man out if she got the chance so she snatched it up and kept low in the bushes.

Time moved as slowly as when a lover waits for another and Tammy struggled to keep breathing. She would forget for moments and then be forced to swallow deep gouts of air which in her ears sounded far too loud for the jungle. When she saw the figure emerge from the bushes her breath caught in her throat and she held it, not daring to breathe. She watched as the small man, sword scabbarded at his waist, moved forward and saw the blood on his grey-green jacket leaking from the tear at his shoulder. The man approached Joelle laid on the stretcher and stared at her. Then he looked up and sniffed. Tammy continued to hold her breath and felt the burn start in her lungs. He sniffed again and looked around then threw a glance back the way he had come and took off into the undergrowth to the right of Tammy. She let her breath out slow and easy, desperately trying to keep quiet. A rustle of leaves caused Tammy to look up again and she watched as Curtis emerged from the same point in the trees as the other man. She wanted to stand but she didn't, fearing the gun that Curtis held. Curtis followed the tracks of the man. He seemed to want to move quickly but held back and took careful steps. He looked at Joelle on the stretcher and then into the bushes where Tammy was hidden. The M1 pointed at the bushes and Tammy watched as Curtis sighted along the barrel.

"Don!"

Curtis threw the barrel skyward.

"Tammy? What the hell are you doing in there?"

She jumped up and stared at him as though he was a mirage created by her fear-addled brain. Curtis looked in the direction the man had taken off in and then snatched Tammy up in his arms. Their mouths met for a moment and they both felt the heat of the other. Tammy pulled away.

"The man, he went into the trees."

"Was he hit?" Curtis stared back down into the trees as they spoke.

"In the shoulder," Tammy jabbed two fingers into her right shoulder.

Curtis nodded.

"Good. I hope the bastard bleeds to death. I found some blood in the trees and he's dropped his rifle. Where are the others?"

"They're going to try and light a beacon up on the mountain. Will shot Joelle."

"What? Why?"

"Because she was slowing him down. Heidi agreed with him but the others didn't. They followed anyway because they were so scared and Will and Heidi had the guns."

"Bastard," muttered Curtis.

"Did you find the others?"

"Samson and Tony. Dead."

Tammy nodded.

"We found what was left of Francesca on the trail. There was another booby trap."

"Benjy?"

Tammy nodded again.

"Well then, that's all of my crew gone."

"What now?"

"Now? I guess we follow Marshall up the mountain. Did you find water?"

A shake of the head and Curtis passed his canteen to Tammy.

"Have as much as you want. There's a stream back in the gully I just came through. We can refill and then carry on."

"Who is he, Don?"

"The man in the jungle? Japanese I reckon, from the rifle I found, maybe a hold-out left over from the war. I heard about some getting found a few years back up around the Phillipines. Didn't think I'd ever run in to one. Either that or some crazy villager who thinks he's a Jap. Not sure it matters really. We just need to stay alive."

"What will you do?"

"When we catch up to Marshall and the rest?"

She nodded.

"Think me and Mr Marshall might have to have a little chat."

14.

Once on the mountain the earth became darker, black and volcanic, and the brush sparser. Marshall and his little group pushed on. They would stop occasionally and share out the contents of one of the vials that Carmine carried. The white powder gave them the energy to push on but it made them hotter and crave, even more, the drinking water that they lacked.

As the sun began to fade they came to more jungle and looking up could see that the mountain proper lay beyond it.

"One more push and I reckon we'll make it."

"Should we take wood from here?" asked Nubia.

Marshall looked at her.

"What?"

"For the beacon, it doesn't look like there'll be much further up on the mountain."

"Good plan, doll," said Carmine, and Marshall nodded.

"Let's get on."

With dry throats and empty stomachs they pushed on into the trees. The fading sun and darker ground made it even more shadowy beneath the canopy than it had been below. Heidi held the big revolver tightly in her fist as she looked from side to side.

"I don't like it in here, it feels wrong."

"I feel you on that," replied Carmine.

Nubia clutched the club she carried to her breast like a hungry infant. Marshall looked around and nodded slowly.

"It feels different doesn't it?"

Nods and murmurs of agreement. As they went forward they moved more slowly looking around constantly in fear of trap or ambush.

"What's that?" asked Heidi pointing the pistol at the shadows below a huge tree whose roots erupted from the dark earth like the legs of some terrible spider.

The rest of the group peered at the murk and saw the shape of something there, the shape of a building. Marshall brought up his pistol and approached the stone walls slowly.

"Some kind of ruins."

Heidi followed and then the others. The walls were made of layers of stone; long slabs sat atop lines of smaller stones and the rest of the stack followed the same pattern. It came up to Marshall's shoulder and was roofless.

"Is this the village?" asked Nubia.

Carmine shook his head.

"I think the sailors said that was down on the coast."

"This is much older," put in Marshall.

"Who built it do you think?" asked Heidi.

Marshall shook his head and ran his hand over the stone.

"I have no idea."

Away from the building stood a tall skinny statue of dark stone that looked something like a man, albeit a strange elongated one. There was something of the Easter Island heads about it but it was skinnier and gaunt with carved eyes that seemed to watch every shadow of the jungle.

The bushes to the right of the structure rustled and the group turned as one. More rustling, growing closer, as something crashed through the jungle towards them. A dark shape half emerged from the bushes when Heidi fired.

The big .357 roared and Marshall's Walther PPK barked twice in response. The shape hurtled forward and Heidi fired again. It slid to a stop in the dark earth leaking blood. They stood around it in a semi-circle and looked down at it – a small, dark, hairy feral boar.

Marshall laughed.

"Looks like we won't be going hungry!"

The sighs of relief were loud and exaggerated. Carmine turned back to the wall and climbed up to look over it.

"You think we should stay here tonight, Will?"

Marshall looked around.

"Be better than being exposed up on the peak."

The two women nodded in agreement. Marshall and Heidi headed into the ruin while Carmine dragged the dead boar after them. Nubia stared for a moment back into the jungle behind them and then followed.

15.

"No way in hell we're going to make that peak before it gets dark."

Tammy nodded. Curtis stepped into the thicker jungle and looked around. He pointed to a tight knot of trees that formed a thicket.

"There."

They walked over and Curtis used his machete to clear some of the bush from inside the thicket. He beat the ground with the blade in an attempt to drive off any snakes or spiders that might be lurking.

"Don't suppose there's any food in that backpack is there?" asked Tammy.

Curtis looked at her and smiled.

"I'm all out of caviar and Bollinger I'm afraid."

Tammy pulled a face.

"I think I'd eat a three day old burrito at this point."

Curtis smiled.

"There're some cans of tuna and one of fruit cocktail."

"Really?"

Curtis continued to smile.

"Might even be a chocolate bar in there somewhere."

They stood for a moment grinning at each other and then Curtis went back to cutting back the bush. Tammy watched the jungle while he worked and held tight to the M1.

*

The gaijin was lucky, that is all. The rifle, which failed me on the beach, is lost. But I still have the sword of my ancestors, my pistol, the weapons the island provides and the last few grenades. If the white devil was lucky then I was luckier still that the bullets he fired passed straight through and did not lodge in my flesh or smash my bones. But still I know I have lost much blood from the wounds. When I arrived back in my camp I was so light headed that I believed that I could see the cherry blossom falling as it did when I was a child and through that blossom walked you my love.

But I must put these thoughts from my mind and focus on stopping the invaders. They are gaining the high ground but the night will be my ally, my cloak and I will wreck much chaos under its veil. The wounds bleed still and they must be stopped. So I take one of the bullets left from the rifle that failed me and empty out the powder, then repeat the process with another. When I have enough powder I grind it finer with the blade of the knife my mother gave me. The Knife I should have used to regain my honour. The powder goes into the wounds and I take a twig from the small fire that I have allowed myself. I breathe as slowly as I can and touch the flame to the back powder. Once in my shoulder and once to the second wound in the meat below my armpit. I feel the powder burn, white hot, and as the pain comes I know I will see you again soon my love.

*

Within the ruin a fire glowed, bigger than it needed to be to cook the skinned boar that was spitted over the flames. Carmine sat looking over the wall with the .357 holstered at his waist and a cigarette between his lips. Tucked against the wall Heidi slept while Nubia watched the cooking meat. Marshall sat alone, smoking, and turning his gun over and over in his hands. The night was like another wall beyond the one built of stone; solid and impenetrable. Carmine flicked his butt into the fire and then dropped down from the wall to stretch his legs.

"Smells good, doll."

Nubia looked at him and smiled.

"I think the sole of a shoe would taste pretty good about now."

"Not unless it was an Ozzie Clark," Carmine replied.

Nubia laughed.

"This is the edge isn't it?"

They stopped talking and looked over at Marshall.

"The fucking edge. Kill or be killed, live or die. Us against him."

"I suppose it is, Will," replied Carmine and Marshall nodded.

"I went to 'Nam you know."

"No, I didn't."

"Yeah, I was *in-country*, took my camera and went out there with the marines. Fuck Curtis. What does he know – Aussies didn't do shit."

Carmine nodded and lit another cigarette. Marshall held up his pistol.

"I'll kill that fucker."

"Curtis?"

"What? No, the one that's out there. *Him*."

"Let's just make sure we get out of here. We'll be leaving too many people on this damned island."

"I think it's ready."

They looked over at Nubia and felt the salivation start anew in their mouths. They crowded around the cooking boar and sniffed up the scent of the sizzling fat. Heidi sat up, the scent of the food having dragged her from sleep. Ignoring the night they clustered around as Nubia lifted the spit away from the flames and prepared to sate their hunger.

*

They are fools who deserve to die. I could smell the cooking meat from the jungle and all I had to do was follow my nose to find them again. There are only four of them and I find myself glad that the tall gaijin with the yellow hair is not amongst them. I curse my cowardly thoughts and drop down onto my belly like the snake that I feel I have become. I can smell the dirt and it makes me glad that I still have the strength to serve

.

16.

The tuna and fruit cocktail were gone the cans empty and licked clean of their juices. Curtis rustled around in his backpack and his hand emerged holding the rich brown wrapper of a Hershey bar. Tammy stared at it for a moment and then he passed it to her.

"Shares?"

Curtis shook his head.

"I don't have much of a sweet tooth, it's all yours," he looked around "I wish we could have a fire but we just can't risk it."

Tammy nodded as she took her first bite of the chocolate.

"Mmmmmm."

"Good?"

Nods in response. Curtis sat and smiled as she ate. He unloaded the clips for the carbine and counted the rounds that he had had left – twenty nine, almost two clips. It would have to do, he thought. He took the sleeping bag from the top of his pack and passed it to Tammy.

"Better try and get your head down for a couple of hours and then take over from me."

Tammy nodded.

"You don't want to climb in for a bit?"

"I couldn't think of anything I'd rather do but it might be a bit risky with our friend around."

Tammy looked around and then wrapped herself in the sleeping bag while Curtis stared out of the thicket at the creeping darkness of the jungle.

*

The boar had been eaten and only the remnants remained. Nubia now wore the gun belt and hefted the .357 in her hand as she walked along the wall, throwing looks at the dark as though she could keep it away by sheer defiance alone. The rest of the group were asleep. Nubia stopped her patrol and thought about home back in Long Island. Since she had got into the modelling it had been a while since she had seen her mother, more than a while, but there under the south Pacific moon she wished she was home, in Yonkers – away from the champagne and cocaine and islands where someone was trying to kill her.

Carmine walked the opposite wall with a club in his hand. Marshall still had his pistol on him even though he was asleep, chin down on his chest. Carmine watched him for a moment and thought about how easy it would be to stroll over and take the gun from Marshall's pocket. He shook the thought from his mind and continued to walk the length of the wall. Heidi was curled up near the fire murmuring as she dreamed.

The nocturnal jungle was alive with sound and Carmine took a second glance at a small tree a little away from the ruins that was shaking.

"What the hell…"

After retrieving a lit branch from the fire Carmine climbed atop the wall and peered out, trying to use the flame to give him more illumination - it marked his position well and as he watched the tree stopped shaking and something long and pale arced through the night. He looked up and watched it descend.

"Oh, fuck!"

The bamboo javelin, its front end weighted by stones bound to it, dropped from the sky and skewered Carmine through his left shoulder. The stones stopped it penetrating more than four or five inches but the blow knocked Carmine off balance and he fell from the wall into the bushes on the other side. The pain from the wound that had been stabbed into his shoulder was intense but Carmine had the strength of mind to hurl the blazing brand away from him. He ducked low and pressed a palm, hard, against the source of the pain. The blood was warm in his hand. There were shouts from inside the camp and Nubia appeared at the wall.

"Watch out," shouted Carmine and another javelin dropped towards the wall.

The javelin shattered on the stone of the wall and Nubia pulled the trigger again and again blasting three bullets out into the night.

"Where is he?" called Marshall.

"Carmine, where are you?" whispered Nubia.

"Not him, the guy throwing the fucking spears."

Carmine grabbed onto the wall and hauled himself up onto it. He stood for a moment and made to jump down into the camp. A flurry of pistol shots erupted in the night kicking shards of stone off of the wall.

"Shit!"

Carmine jumped and landed heavily, falling onto his wounded shoulder with a scream. Marshall fired back, shot after shot, until his clip ran dry. Nubia followed suit and let loose the last three rounds in the .357. Scrambling for the box of shells in his bag Marshall looked over at Carmine who rolled in the dirt. Heidi knelt by the injured man for a moment but when she saw Nubia fumbling with the revolver she took it from her and emptied the spent shells into the dirt. Another pistol shot from out in the dark made them duck down.

"Only eight bullets left, Will."

Heidi held up the gun belt.

"Shit. I've got the better part of the box for this," he held up his own pistol, into which he had just reloaded a freshly charged clip "you think you can keep him pinned down while I work around his flank?"

Heidi nodded.

"Yes."

She leaned against the wall, keeping low so that just her eyes and the top of her head peeked over. She watched the jungle for a few moments and was rewarded with the flash of a muzzle in the dark. The bullet flew high and blew a chunk from a tree on the far side of the ruin.

"I see him."

Marshall nodded and then looked at his hands. He realised he was shaking but wiped the sweat from his palms off on his shorts and picked up his pistol. Nubia looked up from where she was kneeling down with Carmine.

"Be careful, Will."

He nodded once and then slipped through a gap in the wall and out into the night. Heidi rested the barrel of the .357 on the wall and took careful aim at the spot where she had seen the muzzle flash and then she fired.

*

The ripple of shots echoed down the mountain to where Curtis and Tammy were bivouacked. Curtis grabbed the M1 and climbed out of the thicket. He pushed through the trees and looked up to where the sounds had come from. Even from so far back down he could see the glow of the fire amongst, and above, the trees.

"Shit,"

"What?"

"They're in trouble."

"You think we should go up there?"

Curtis shook his head.

"It'd be suicide in the dark. Might not spot any traps and might run in to him on the way."

But still Curtis stood staring.

"You want to go?"

He nodded.

"I can't leave them. Too many dead already."

Tammy retrieved the back pack and pulled it on.

"I'll carry this, let's go."

Curtis looked up from checking the M1.

"You're a good woman, Tammy Rodriguez."

She smiled back.

"When we get out of here I might make you do something about that."

They headed off towards the fire and the place from where the shots still sounded.

17.

After her fourth shot Heidi paused and waited. There had been no shots fired back in response. She stared out into the dark and tried to see where Marshall was. Carmine's shoulder was bound up with torn strips of his shirt, the medical kit still with Tammy.

"Anything?"

Heidi reloaded the pistol with the last of the bullets.

"Four bullets left."

"The box Will left?" asked Nubia.

Heidi shrugged.

"When these are gone we can see if they fit."

*

Marshall kept low and crept forward. He stopped and listened for a moment but heard nothing except the usual sounds of the jungle before the night was split by Heidi firing off another round.

"Good girl," he whispered to himself "keep the bastard's head down."

He brought up the Walther and pushed on. Leaves and branches grabbed at him as Marshall stepped through the foliage. He strained his eyes watching for movement. Heidi's pistol was silent and Marshall worried that his adversary could have got around him and into the camp. He was trying to decide whether to carry on or head back when he sensed something to his rear. He froze and then turned his head. The man stood about ten yards away, shadowed by the trees but Marshall could clearly see the pistol pointed at his back. The short man smiled and pulled the trigger. The click made Marshall flinch and the man stare at his weapon. The man looked back up and hurled the pistol at Marshall's back but the photographer was already moving.

Once behind a tree Marshall turned and fired. His wild shot went high but the other man ducked into the bushes, out of sight. Marshall stepped out and fired off another two rounds into the bushes. He waited for a moment with his gun sighted on the spot where the man had been. Seconds ticked away. Marshall took a step back towards camp and then another. A blood-curdling scream away to his right made Marshall turn and he saw the man rushing from the trees with his sword held high.

"Baaaaaaaaaaanzai!"

"Oh, shit!"

Marshall snapped off a shot and then ran. His knees pumped high and he ducked beneath branches and hurdled logs. The man pursuing him continued to scream but Marshall dared not risk a look back. When he reached the break in the wall he turned and fired again but the man was not behind him. Marshall scanned the jungle and felt the shakes come back into his hands. He stepped back through the break in the wall and kept his pistol trained on the gap.

Nubia rushed over, Carmine leaned up against the wall and Heidi simply threw a look over before going back to watching the dark.

*

Progress was slow through the night as Curtis moved with extra care and paused regularly to check for booby traps. His persistence paid off when he found two pits filled with sharpened stakes covered with rugs of woven grass. Curtis nodded once to Tammy and then moved back to point.

They found the hollow in the early hours of pale light. It was just off the trail.

"Looks like it was dug out."

"By him?"

Curtis nodded and pushed away the branches and leaves carefully. The bones and skulls were just beneath the surface.

"Oh, my God. Are those other people that he has killed?"

Curtis picked up a long bone from a leg and looked it over; smooth with tiny tool marks on it. He threw the bone back into the hollow. In with the bones he could see pieces of rotted uniform and a white and red flag.

"Shit."

"What?" asked Tammy.

"He ate them."

"Who?"

"The other soldiers that were with him; the bones are smooth where he boiled them and the tool marks are from where he picked the meat off with a knife or something."

"Jesus! So we're dealing with a cannibal?"

Curtis shook his head.

"These aren't recent. I think he ate them early on before he knew how to get food from the island. Maybe he ate them as they died. My uncle told me stories about what he saw out on the Kokoda trail."

"Where was that?"

Curtis laughed.

"Where us Aussies finally held the Japs. Well before Iwo Jima or Guadalcanal. He told us they'd find little pockets of cut-off Japanese troops who had taken to eating the dead. Said they shot them where they found them."

They walked away from the hollow and its ghosts, back to the trail, and Tammy reached for Curtis' hand.

*

By the time they got close to the ruin dawn was beginning to colour the sky and a mist hung close to the floor of the jungle. Curtis stared at the crude statue that seemed to watch him from the gloom of the trees.

"Stay close," Curtis whispered and moved towards the walls.

They had only gone a few paces when gunfire punched out at them - three shots in quick succession. Curtis pushed Tammy down and ducked low with the M1 aimed at the wall.

"It's Curtis. I've got Tammy with me," he shouted.

He waited and could hear low voices behind the wall.

"If that's you Marshall let me know or I'm going to start shooting at the next thing I see moving."

"It's us," shouted Carmine in response.

"Okay. We're coming in. Hold your fire – okay?"

"Okay!" came the response.

Curtis stood up and helped Tammy to her feet.

"Like I said before – you stay close."

Tammy nodded and they moved together towards the ruin.

18.

Curtis stood with the butt of the carbine resting on his hip, Tammy hung back behind him. He looked over what was left of the group; Heidi by the wall with the .357, Carmine bandaged up, Nubia looking drawn and scared and Marshall standing with the small automatic in his hand watching Curtis.

"Did you find the others?"

Curtis nodded.

"Dead. I hear you found Francesca?"

"Yes, booby trapped and died with your man."

"See Joelle didn't make it either."

Marshall stared straight at Curtis.

"No, she succumbed to her wounds on the way up the mountain."

Carmine and Nubia looked at the photographer. He continued to watch Curtis.

"Not quite the way I heard it."

Marshall looked past Curtis at Tammy.

"Bitch, what the hell have you said?"

The barrel of the carbine swung to point at Marshall's chest and Curtis brought up his left hand to steady the weapon.

"Best we keep it civil don't you think?"

Marshall stepped back and raised his hands, gun still in his right.

"Carmine, you mind taking that off Mr Marshall before someone else *succumbs*?"

Carmine took the pistol in his good hand and stepped back. Curtis and Marshall eyed each other.

"Think you'd better hand that big pistol over too, Heidi."

The blonde woman considered the gun in Curtis' hands for a moment before she slid the .357 back into its holster and undid the gun belt. She stepped forward and held it out. Tammy took the pistol.

"Put it on," said Curtis and Tammy complied "now does someone want to tell me what happened last night?"

Marshall had walked away to stare over the wall into the jungle lighting one of his few remaining cigarettes and Heidi went to stand with him. Carmine spoke first and then Nubia joined in. They ran down the events of the night before for the Captain up until Marshall's escape from the sword-wielding assailant. After that they had stayed within the ruins, staying awake and keeping constant watch on all sides.

"So what now?" asked Nubia.

Curtis shrugged.

"Same plan as far as I see it – we take the high ground and get the beacon lit."

Marshall laughed.

"Got something to add, *Mister* Marshall?"

"You think he'll let us get up there? Shit, how many us of are already dead?"

Curtis looked away.

"You and your men were meant to look after us."

Curtis looked up, anger in his eyes.

"My men have paid with their lives you prick!"

Marshall sucked on his cigarette and turned away.

"I'm going up that mountain and I'm lighting a beacon, after that we wait."

"Food, water? It's all down here in the jungle where *he* is. Did you file a route of where we were going?" Marshall had turned and walked back towards Curtis stabbing his cigarette in the air to emphasise his points.

Curtis thought for a moment about the permanently drunk harbour master back in the port and shook his head.

"No, I didn't."

Marshall was right and Curtis knew it, once they were on the peak they would be exposed to the sun and would need water and food if they were to wait for help. He thought for a few moments and then nodded to himself.

"You're right, Marshall. We build the beacon and see if we can spot the village that used to be here. Get down there and see if we can salvage something to make a raft. Then, while the beacon burns, we head back towards the main islands and hope someone meets us on the way."

Marshall stood and considered what Curtis had said before finally nodding.

"Now that sounds like a plan. Get off this godforsaken rock and away from that maniac with the sword," he looked Curtis in the eye for a moment "Jap you think?"

Curtis nodded.

"Looks like it. He dropped his rifle and I know the type – an Arisaka rifle. My Uncle had one that he took off a Nip on the Kokoda Trail."

"Think he's been out here all that time, thirty five years?" asked Nubia.

"Starting to look that way, enough to drive anyone round the bend," replied Curtis.

Carmine sat down on a log, pistol dangling in his fist. Curtis passed his canteen to the little man.

"Thanks,"

"No problem. You okay?"

Carmine nodded.

"Like I said I'm from Brooklyn – I've been stabbed before."

Curtis couldn't help but smile.

"Really?"

"Yeah, drag queen from over in Greenpoint took a dislike to me."

"Shit,"

Curtis laughed and Carmine joined in.

"Hurts like a bitch but I know it'll be okay. Has to be okay. I won't slow you down."

"Don't worry about it, I'll get Heidi to carry you if I have to. You check the tip of the spear or whatever it was he threw?"

Carmine shook his head.

"He threw another after - it's over there somewhere. Why should I have checked…ah shit – the shit."

Curtis patted him on his good shoulder and went to find the javelin. In the daylight that managed to penetrate the canopy it was easy enough to find. Curtis picked it up; the tip was fire hardened but there was no evidence of the faeces that had coated the stakes in the traps they had found. He walked back and showed it to Carmine.

"Looks clean enough. You ready to get to the top of this place?"

Carmine nodded, tucked Marshall's pistol into the top of his shorts and let Curtis haul him up onto his feet.

"Yeah, I can make it. Show you what us Brooklyn boys can do."

As he followed Curtis, Carmine looked back and saw Marshall watching him. He checked the gun was secure in his waist and stared back at Marshall, the flesh in his shoulder screaming as it tried to knit itself back together.

19.

It is so long since I have spoken to another soul, except for the ghosts which dwell in my own thoughts and the demons which haunt my dreams. The men I once served with surround me in my dreams – they are a part of me now. I think of the gaijins *on my island and wish that one of them had a few words of my language; just a sentence or two – anything, a word even. Traitorous thoughts! Put them away and drag myself from the nest I had cocooned myself in for a few hours of sleep. I look at the sword of my ancestors. It and the weapons the island provides me with are the only ones that have not failed me. The grenades are gone now. Six of my enemies left. I pray that enough strength remains in this weak vessel to take them. Strap my sword on once more and promise it the heads of my enemies.*

*

Soon the jungle gave way to bare, black rock and the sun beat down harder than before now that they were clear of the protective canopy of the jungle that lay below. They had hacked down branches and gathered as much loose timber as they could before bundling it with vines and dragging it towards the peak. Curtis stayed at the back watching the tree-line with his carbine at the ready. Nothing stirred within the trees but he continued to watch until the group were well clear.

They pushed on and, just before the sun reached its peak, they crested the rise to the top of the mountain. Tammy stopped and wiped the sweat from her forehead. She looked out and took in the vista that the mountain top provided – the endless sea, and in that never ending blue she realised just how far they were from anywhere. The tears came before she could stop them.

Marshall started piling the wood quickly and Carmine watched him carefully. Heidi and Nubia helped to pile the branches and sticks into, what looked to Carmine to be, a funeral pyre. Curtis moved to Tammy and squeezed her shoulder. She nodded and sniffed back the tears.

"Let's get this started," said Marshall lighting his last cigarette.

Curtis nodded and lit a cigarette of his own.

"We wait till it's a proper blaze, I'm not having our little friend coming up to kick it apart."

"Agreed."

Curtis piled the kindling beneath the branches and Marshall sparked the wheel of his

Ronson. The flame took and they watched it lick at the wood. The smoke came first and then the flames. They waited and watched as the fire took hold. Curtis threw handfuls of leaves that he had collected amongst the wood.

"Smoke might help. That way even if they don't see the flames they might think this old fella is setting to erupt again and sail over to take a look."

Carmine was looking out over the island when he caught sight of the ramshackle, broken-down huts on the far coast.

"The village,"

Curtis walked over and followed Carmine's pointed finger. He nodded and called the others over.

"That's where we're heading. If anyone is separated you just head for the shoreline and follow it back to the village – got it?"

They nodded and Curtis held up the M1.

"How are we doing for ammo?"

"Only two in this," said Tammy.

"Full clip and Marshall has more in his bag," added Carmine.

Curtis held out his hand and Marshall retrieved the box from his camera bag and passed it over. There were twenty or so nine millimetre shells in the box. Carmine managed to stuff the box into his pocket and they looked to the trees that hid the route to the village.

"You think he's down there waiting?" asked Tammy.

"I have no doubts on that," replied Curtis "I'll take point, Carmine you'll have to take drag."

Carmine nodded, too tired to even crack a joke, and then Marshall spoke.

"Come on, he's hurt. I should be bringing up the back."

Curtis' smile was thin when he spoke.

"Think I'd trust you behind me with a pistol? Carmine, you reckon you can handle it?"

Carmine looked up and blinked his eyes back into focus.

"Brooklyn all the way. I ain't down until I'm down," his voice was slow and his accent was slipping to something that sounded more like it was from the place he had been raised.

Curtis leaned in close to Tammy.

"Watch Carmine, I think he's hurt worse than he's letting on," then he raised his voice so everyone could hear "keep your eyes open and move slow. We take our time and all get down to the village, get out of this place."

Once everyone had nodded their affirmation Curtis turned and jogged ahead. Marshall looked over at Carmine and wondered how long the little man could stay on his feet and he watched the gun, his gun, tucked in the waistband of his shorts.

*

They are coming and I wait once more. I wait and watch. I watch the shape of their movement. See the man at the back moving slower than the rest and see the woman who watches him. Three guns while I have none. But I have my sword, my honour, my duty and my memories. Memories that must be washed clean with blood, to remove the stain from my honour. When I see my ancestors again it will be as equals.

20.

Putting one foot in front of the other, Carmine tried to keep pace with the rest. He realised he wasn't watching the jungle like he was meant to and stopped, pulling the pistol from his waist. He looked around but nothing seemed out of place. After nodding once to himself he tucked the pistol back into his waistband and went back to putting one foot in front of the other.

Curtis stopped. He held his hand up to halt the others and then stepped off to the side of the trail he was following. After moving some way into the bushes he found footprints in the dirt. Looked at them – fresh? He couldn't tell. It had been too long since he had tracked another man. Once he was back with the others he lifted his hand and signalled for them to follow.

Carmine walked with his eyes closed as fresh pain blossomed beneath the makeshift bandages. One foot in front of the other. The pain began to fade and then he wasn't walking on dark volcanic dirt any longer but the solid grey concrete at La Guardia, coming back from a trip with Will. Through the airport and into a yellow cab. Home, James. Stop in at his mother's house; Veal Parmesan, pasta with a pork and beef gravy, fresh bread from *Giovanni's Bakery* on the corner - all of it. Then hop another cab over to the Village and go cruising. Carmine smiled as he walked. Heard his name called and wasn't sure whether it was from the leather boy at the bar in his mind or the reality he kept his eyes closed against.

"Carmine, where are you going?"

The pain came back in waves and reminded Carmine where he was. He opened his eyes and looked around. He had wandered away from the direction that the others had taken and Tammy had come after him. *Gidrul'*, he cursed himself and tried to focus. He took another step and felt his foot come down on something tense and taut. Looking down he saw the vine give and his eyes tried to follow where the line went. Movement above him in the tree tops made him look up just in time for him to see the tree stump hurtling towards him. Carmine managed a half shuffle to the right but it was too late. The stump came down faster than the L-train going along Bedford Avenue and hit him in the chest, throwing him back like a rag doll hurled by a toddler in a tantrum as the stump continued its arc. He lay on the ground for a moment. The wind had been knocked out of him and he knew that things inside him were broken, for sure, but he was alive. He rolled up onto his knees.

"Carmine! No, get down!" Tammy screamed at him.

Carmine turned and watched the tree stump coming down on its backswing. He watched as the lump of wood raced towards his face. It was as though the tree stump's descent had hypnotised him and he did not move as it struck him full in the face, his head came apart like a balloon filled with red paint being hit with a bat. Carmine's body stayed on its knees for a moment pumping blood out through what was left of his ruined neck before toppling to rest in the dark dirt.

The tree stump continued to swing, slowing with each pendulation. Tammy ran close and looked at what was left of Carmine. Marshall joined her.

"Shit," he muttered "he deserved better than that."

Marshall caught the swinging stump and halted its motion. He reached down and retrieved his Walther and the box of ammunition, checked there was a round in the chamber and kept it in his hand rather than tucking it into his pocket. Curtis walked over slowly and swore under his breath. Heidi and Nubia gathered around and they looked down at what was left of the little dresser from Brooklyn.

*

They didn't bury Carmine or even move his body. They left him where he lay and pushed on deeper into the jungle towards the village on the coast. Curtis saw the gun in Marshall's hand but said nothing. There was death in the air and Curtis wouldn't wish anyone to be unarmed. Heidi held a machete, Nubia a club. Tammy left the .357 and its two remaining shots in its holster. They paused on the trail and Curtis shared around his canteen. He offered a cigarette to Marshall who took it gladly.

"Anyone else?"

Nubia took one while Heidi and Tammy shook their heads. Curtis sparked the smokes.

"How much further do you think?" asked Marshall.

"We keep up the pace and avoid any more surprises and we should reach the village before dark."

Nubia shuddered and then held herself.

"I don't want to spend another night in the open."

Tammy nodded.

"You've got that right. Four walls and a roof."

"Not sure we'll get that but hopefully something defensible will still be standing."

"Want me to take point?" asked Tammy and Curtis shook his head in response.

"No. I've done this before. It's best that it's me."

He finished his cigarette and strapped the canteen back to his belt before jogging on ahead.

*

And six become five. They fall like the blossoms from the trees. They are heading towards the place where I learnt the truth about betrayal. Perhaps I will let them pass in peace so that they can see that I know the truth. Perhaps. If the island does not kill them all before they get that far.

21.

The village came into view as the sun began to drop to the horizon. Five houses, or at least their walls, remained standing. The others had fallen in on themselves in the years of neglect that had followed the exodus from the small fishing village. Curtis immediately checked for any boats that might have remained behind but apart from one severely rotted canoe there was nothing.

They picked the strongest looking house, one that had half a tin roof left, and moved inside. The food from Curtis' rucksack was long gone. There were a few greasy pieces of meat that Nubia had wrapped in the cloth of her sarong. The five survivors wolfed it down.

"There has to be a stream near here," said Curtis "stands to reason, they wouldn't build a village otherwise."

"Why do you think they left?" asked Heidi.

"Our *friend* in the jungle?" added Marshall.

Curtis nodded.

"Could well be. He bothered them for enough years and they might have left."

"You want me to go and look for this stream?" asked Marshall.

Curtis nodded again.

"Thanks."

"No problem. I'll take Heidi with me."

Marshall gestured at Heidi and they left the house.

"I'm going to check the other houses," said Curtis.

He left Tammy and Nubia together and headed out towards the remnants of the other buildings. Once Curtis was gone Nubia looked at Tammy.

"You think we're going to make it?"

"Of course we will. I'm not going to die on some piss-ant island in the middle of nowhere."

Nubia smiled.

"I just want to go home."

"I know what you mean."

"I don't just mean back to the States. I mean away from all this. Back to where I'm from."

Tammy nodded.

"You got that straight – think Will will let us go?"

Tammy had said it with a smile on her lips but Nubia looked back with fear.

"You won't say anything about Joelle, will you?"

"What do you mean?"

"Will won't want anyone knowing about that will he?"

Tammy shook her head and thought on it.

"No, I don't suppose he will."

*

The roof of the first house, along with one of its walls had collapsed in on itself. Curtis stepped inside and looked around. Nothing. He moved out and headed to the next building. As soon as he stepped through what was left of the door Curtis knew that there was something different here. He kept the carbine held at waist level and moved further inside. The remains of the roof had been positioned to provide some shelter to one corner of the main room. He ducked low and, in the falling dark, wished that he had a torch as he crept forward. In the failing light Curtis saw a threadbare blanket, a pile of fish bones and a metal tin. He stared at the tin for a moment before deciding it was too small to contain a grenade. He slid the knife from the sheath on his belt and felt around the box for triggers and wires. There were none. Curtis lifted the tin and popped the lid, all the while expecting an explosion to take his hands. The lid fell to the floor and Curtis looked at the documents inside. They were written on paper that seemed as thin as onion skin and in a language that Curtis couldn't read. It looked like Japanese but he could not be sure. Curtis stared at them for a moment, they could be love letters from back home or military secrets – did it matter anymore? Curtis put the letters back and popped the lid back on. Another look around the den showed the newspaper covers stuck to the wall; a picture of a mushroom cloud, JAPAN SURRENDERS! screamed a headline, VJ DAY proclaimed another. Even if you couldn't read the words the pictures were clear – capitulation, the Japanese delegation standing with their heads down. Curtis stepped back. He thought of the other Japanese hold-outs that had been found claiming that the war hadn't finished and that they had had to fight on. He looked at the newspapers and they sent a shudder through him. The man on the island must know that the war was finished, that it had finished a long time ago. Curtis took another look at the headlines and then headed back to the house that they had claimed as their own.

*

The stream was easy enough to find. Marshall dropped to his knees and lapped at the water like a dog before a toilet. Heidi followed suit and fell down onto her belly to lap up the water. They looked at each other and laughed.

"All this water just makes me feel dirtier," said Heidi.

Marshall nodded.

"I know just what you mean. Why don't I go and fill the bottles further upstream and you can bathe in the pool."

"Really, Will? That would be wonderful. To be clean again!"

Marshall smiled and carried the water bottles further up the stream towards the tree-line, pistol in his hand and an eye on the trees. He kneeled down, putting the gun on the ground next to him, and began filling the first bottle, all the time continuing to watch the jungle.

Heidi stripped off her shirt and shorts so that all she wore was her black bikini. She stepped into the fresh water – it was a lot colder than the sea was but she smiled at the bite of it. It made her remember the streams in the Austrian Tyrol when she was growing up; they had been much colder, snow-cold in the spring. She pushed off into the pool and spun in the water so that she lay on her back looking up. The stars glittered bright and proud in the pure night above her. She rubbed her hands over herself and within moments felt the dirt and sweat drop away. She ducked her head under the water and came up gasping.

A bird call made Marshall drop the bottle he was filling and grab for his pistol. He held the gun for a moment and it calmed him, when the fear rescinded he put the Walther back down and resumed filling the bottles. Marshall wished he had a cigarette and decided he'd ask Curtis once he got back with the water.

The water cleansed and Heidi smiled.

"It's wonderful, Will. You should get in!"

Marshall looked up and smiled.

"Maybe I will once I'm done."

Heidi smiled and spun herself around in the water once again. She stared at the single cane that stood up in the water, so out of place. She watched as it moved towards her and she felt the fingers of fear push their way inside her. With slow movements she headed for the bank. She gripped it and pulled herself out of the pool. She was halfway out when the water behind her erupted. Risking a look back she saw the man, cane tube still between his lips and the glittering blade of his sword.

"No," she said quietly and the man lunged.

The folded steel bit into her between her legs and slid deep. Heidi screamed and Marshall turned from filling the bottles. He watched as the sword vanished inside Heidi. The man turned and smiled at him as he lifted Heidi off the ground with force of his thrust, twisted the blade and then hurled her aside, the blade sliding out and looking black in the moonlight.

"Shit,"

Marshall fumbled for the Walther but the man was already moving, so light on his feet. He leaped from the pool onto the bank and pointed the katana straight at Marshall. The pistol seemed to snake away from Marshall's grasp and by the time he had it, solid in his grip, and had looked back the man had vanished. Marshall screamed and fired a single impotent shot into the air. He grabbed up the canteens and walked over to where Heidi lay. She moaned and looked up at Marshall, blood smeared down the insides of her legs as she writhed in the dirt.

"It hurts, Will. So bad. "

Marshall kneeled down and stroked her golden hair.

"Please, Will. Kill me – it hurts too much."

Marshall looked away and thought about the bullet he had put into Joelle. He looked down at her again and felt tears prick his eyes. Footfalls sounded and Marshall turned his head. When he saw it was the others coming he looked back to Heidi and was amazed at how pale she had become.

"Shit, where is he?" asked Curtis.

Marshall shook his head.

"I don't know. He was there and then he was gone. I think he was hiding under the water."

"Let's get her back to the house," said Nubia.

"No… Please. The pain. So much pain. End it here."

"We can help you," said Tammy but the lie died on her lips when she looked more closely at the terrible wound that had been inflicted on Heidi and the amount of blood that had already soaked into the dirt.

Marshall looked at Curtis, tears streaming down his cheeks. Curtis looked at the blood in the dirt and then nodded. Nubia and Tammy took Heidi's hands and held them tight as Marshall stood up and aimed the Walther at her head. He took a breath and looked away as he squeezed the trigger.

22.

Silence reigned in the ruined house. Curtis crouched by a window keeping watch on the jungle while Tammy and Nubia clung together beneath his sleeping bag. There was no fire and Marshall sat alone smoking one of Curtis' cigarettes. He kept the Walther close by his hand as he smoked. Heidi's body lay in the corner covered by a blanket – they had not wanted to leave it outside.

"Want me to take a watch?"

Curtis looked over at Marshall.

"Sure."

"You need to sleep, you've been trying to look after us since yesterday."

"Thanks," replied Curtis passing the M1 to Marshall, getting the Walther in return.

"You think we're right to go?"

"To build a raft and get the hell off this island?"

Marshall nodded.

"Why wouldn't we be?"

"Maybe we should stay and stop him."

Curtis stared at the photographer - for a moment similar thoughts had dogged his own mind.

"Just us?" he replied finally.

"You think the people who lived here tried to stop him?"

Curtis nodded.

"Yeah, I would've thought they would have tried. Machetes and a couple of homemade guns against him out there in that green hell."

"And he's still here."

"We get back and we can get the army called out. Let them hunt that bastard down."

Marshall nodded but Curtis could see he wasn't convinced. Curtis clapped a hand on his shoulder and handed over the last pack of cigarettes.

"Wake me up in a couple of hours and then get your head down yourself."

Turning to the window Marshall stared out at the jungle and wondered if their enemy was watching them right now. Marshall lit a cigarette and continued to keep watch.

*

Tammy awoke in the half-light before the dawn and saw Marshall sitting at the window. She climbed out from beneath Nubia's arm and walked over to him.

"How are you doing, Will?"

Marshall seemed not to hear her so intently was he watching the tree-line.

"Will?"

"What, sorry?" he replied turning.

She smiled at him.

"I said how are you doing?"

"Not so good," he replied.

"Heidi?"

He nodded.

"And Joelle and Carmine and Francesca and Tony and the others. They deserved better, better than what they got."

"You can't think like that, Will. Not now. Not till we get out of here and then you can feel as guilty as you want to."

He looked over at Curtis, curled up and asleep.

"You think anything will come of it if we get out of here?"

"He's a good man."

Marshall nodded.

"He is. Things got a bit crazy up on the mountain."

Tammy shook her head.

"You don't need to say it, Will. What happened up there wasn't real life – it was survival pure and simple. Joelle was already dead, same as Heidi. You just helped them on their way."

Marshall forced a twisted version of his oh-so white smile.

"You think it'll be any different today, you think that bastard will let us go this easily?"

"We haven't gone anywhere yet."

Marshall looked back to the trees.

"All night I could feel his eyes on us. It isn't right that he's alive and all those others are dead."

"We have to survive, Will. That's all we can do."

Tammy went to Curtis, ducked down and shook his shoulder. He was awake instantly, hand going to the Walther.

"It's almost morning, Don."

"Thank you," he replied shaking the sleep from his head "You see anything, Mr Marshall?"

Marshall laughed.

"Call me Will, please. No, nothing but he's out there - I know he is."

Curtis passed the pistol back and slung the carbine over his shoulder.

"I think we best start looking for a way to get this raft made."

*

By mid-morning they had collected and piled the materials for the raft on the beach. Marshall had kept watch while they searched. The search had turned up plenty of timber and sheet metal from the roofs as well as six large metal drums. Curtis looked them over and Marshall walked over from where he had been keeping guard.

"Will it work?"

Curtis nodded as he looked over the pile.

"I think it will. Tammy, I need Will to help me," he passed the carbine to her.

She headed off to watch the jungle. Nubia looked down the beach.

"There're some rock pools not far. I could go and see if there's anything – clams, crabs."

"You need to be careful."

"I know that. I've seen what that bastard has done."

Marshall passed her the Walther.

"Take that."

"Thank you, Will."

The two men watched her walk along the sand with trepidation in their hearts. It was Marshall who broke the silence.

"This raft isn't going to build itself."

"More's the pity," replied Curtis and they set to work.

The raft came together quickly; using some rusty cable, forgotten rope and vines from nearby bushes they lashed together a wood frame over the six old oil drums. The corrugated steel sheeting was then added as a deck. Curtis and Marshall stepped back and admired their work.

"Two cigarettes left," said Marshall.

Curtis smiled.

"Smoke 'em if you got 'em."

They stood and smoked looking the raft over.

"And you're sure it'll float?"

"Float?" replied Curtis "it had better fucking float."

Nubia came back along the beach with three dead coconut crabs, shells smashed by the club, dangling from her fist.

"Time to eat before we get the hell out of here?"

Stomachs grumbled and mouths salivated.

"Be stupid not to," replied Curtis.

*

I watch the cowards build their little raft and I smile. Soon the island will be mine again – just mine. They must have found the small camp that I kept in the ruins and if they did then they know the truth. That it was my decision to remain here and never go back to the land that betrayed me – betrayed my Emperor, my honour and everything it was that I fought for.

I never surrendered but they did. Cowards.

If I still had my rifle I would fire at them and hurry their way off the island. I retrieved the rifle but my clever, clever enemy had taken the bolt from it.

I see them build their fire and cook the crabs that the black one found in the pools. I am loath to let them go. My only companions since I drove the villagers away so many years ago. I sigh. Death would be a release but I gave my word to myself that I would not and so, I will not.

23.

According to Curtis' watch it was just after one in the afternoon when they launched the raft into the shallows. Marshall and the women were on the raft clutching crudely crafted paddles. Curtis stayed in the water and pushed the raft further out. When he got to the point where his toes dragged on the sand he reached up and let Marshall haul him up onto the metal deck.

"We're really getting away!" shouted Nubia.

Curtis grabbed up the paddle he had hacked from a plank and dug into the water. The others did the same and they propelled the raft away from the beach.

"We'll try and follow the coast around the island."

The others nodded and they continued to paddle until they were a hundred yards or so off the beach. Curtis and Tammy paddled on one side turning the raft and then they moved away off up the coast.

"Watch the beach, he might have had more than one rifle," said Curtis and Marshall threw eyes at the shore.

A little water slopped up onto the deck but the raft seemed to be holding together. Curtis had the M1 carbine slung high on his back away from the water. As much as they paddled they seemed to be drawn back towards the island.

"Is it the tide?" asked Tammy and Curtis nodded in response.

"Hopefully we can use it. Let it propel us along the edge of the island then fight through it with a bit of elbow grease."

They took their paddles out of the water and the tide pulled them along. The raft ran close to the island but they were still thirty yards off the beach. The speed increased and the raft moved along at a good pace. Curtis watched and could see it being drawn into towards the rocks of the coast.

"Shit, we need to start paddling like hell before we get dashed onto those rocks!"

Everyone dug in and dug deep trying to propel the raft back towards the open ocean. But no matter how hard they worked the raft moved towards the rocks like an iron filing drawn towards a magnet. And then, with a heaving wrench, the raft hit something just below the water. A drum was torn loose and the raft dipped. Tammy fell forward and Curtis grabbed the waistband of her shorts hauling her back. With one drum torn away the raft began to work loose from itself as it closed in on the rocks. Curtis let go of his makeshift paddle and made sure that his grip on Tammy was tight as he grabbed the far edge of the deck.

The raft struck with jarring force and began to come apart, falling into pieces. Nubia was thrown out onto the rocks and Marshall dived to try and grab her ankle. He missed and she was thrown clear. The raft pulled back and then clattered into the rocks once more. Curtis scrambled up, pulling Tammy with him, as the remnants of the raft slid away. They leapt for the rocks in the moment before the raft struck again and truly came apart. They hit the rocks hard. Tammy had a tight grip on Curtis' rucksack but the Captain felt the sling of the carbine snag on something and tighten against him before it tore.

"No!" he shouted as the M1 slipped down the rocks and vanished into the angry waters.

Marshall fell into the water and a piece of the deck struck him in the head. He went down for a moment but came up spluttering, blood streaming from a shallow gash across his forehead. The waves plucked at him and threw him against the rocks. Marshall grunted against the pain of his flesh being dragged down the rocks but he scrambled and grabbed at a handhold. His fingers found purchase and he pulled himself clear of the raging waters.

Nubia got up and walked a few steps before she stumbled and fell. She pushed herself back up and walked towards the trees at the edge of the rocks. She could feel the warm blood leaking down her legs from dozens of scratches from where she had landed on the rocks. Her head span and the greenery before her swam. She reached up and felt the swollen lump on the side of her head. The sword blade fired out from amongst the foliage and its tip smashed teeth as it punched through her mouth and out the back of her skull. In one swift moment the sword was withdrawn with a spatter of blood across the rocks. Nubia reached for the Walther she had pushed into her pocket. She got the gun clear and thumbed back the hammer as she tried to focus. The man stepped from the bushes and looked at her for a moment. She made to raise the pistol but the sword blade lanced out, a glitter of steel in the afternoon sun, and across her throat. The pistol fell from her hand as she threw her hands up to the wound at her throat. She turned back towards the sea and walked away.

Tammy looked up and saw Nubia walking towards her. A smile leapt to her lips.

"You're okay?"

Then she saw the blood oozing from between Nubia's fingers and her smile fell away. Nubia made to say something and raised her head, the action made her chin tip skyward and her head to fall back tearing what little sinew and gristle held it to the stump of her neck. Nubia's head bounced down the rocks past Tammy and plopped into the sea.

*

"Where's the Walther?" whispered Curtis.

Marshall shook his head.

"I let Nubia hold onto it."

"Jesus…"

Tammy drew the .357 and held it out towards Curtis. Curtis took the pistol and opened the cylinder – two shells remained.

"You still got the rest of the ammo, Will?"

Marshall nodded and pulled the sodden cardboard box from his pocket. .380 cartridges spilled out onto the rocks. Curtis picked one up and tried to fit it into the cylinder. It was just too large to fit.

"Shit."

He handed the gun to Marshall.

"I'm going to have to go down after the carbine."

"Don, no it's too dangerous."

A wave crashed against the rocks as though to illustrate Tammy's point but Curtis shook his head.

"We have to have it. Will, you watch our front but hold your fire unless you're sure."

Marshall nodded. Curtis moved to the edge of the rocks and slipped down into the water. He felt the pull of the current as soon as he was in. Felt himself being pulled out and then sucked back in towards the rocks. He waited until the current pulled him out again and then dived beneath the surface. The water was cloudy here as the sand was kicked up and lashed against the rocks. Curtis pushed on until his hand grasped at the bottom. He felt his way around until his lungs burned. He turned and kicked off the bottom. Bursting out of the water Curtis sucked in great gasps of air. The water plucked him and forced him against the rocks, tearing at the flesh of his flank. Tammy was down on her belly watching for him.

"Anything?"

Curtis managed to shake his head. He sucked in more air and then went back under, pushing hard with his legs to propel himself towards the bottom. His search was, once again, fruitless and he returned to the surface empty handed. His battle against the currents had sapped his strength and Tammy half-dragged him back up onto the rocks.

"What are we going to do, Don?"

Curtis looked up at the blue sky and tried to think.

A shot sounded and a chunk of rock was chipped away in front of Marshall. The photographer flattened himself against the rock and tried to work out where the shot had come from.

"How many were left in the clip?" shouted Curtis.

"Six."

"Then he's down to five."

Curtis risked a look over the rocks at the tree-line. He looked at Marshall.

"We need to get out of here before he works out that we haven't got the M1. I'm going to make a run for the trees over there," Curtis pointed "and try to get him to waste those shots. You watch and see if you can pinpoint his position. Let him have one round and then save the other – unless you're sure that you can put him down."

Marshall nodded, wiped his hands on his shorts and then took up the .357 in a two handed grip. Curtis moved forward in a crouch and then burst out of the rocks running for the trees. He heard the first short and dirt kicked up behind him. *Four*. Curtis dinked to the right and tried to make himself small as he ran. Another shot, this one close enough that Curtis heard it zing through the air close to him. *Three*. Curtis threw himself to the ground and then jumped up for his final dash into the trees. Bark was blown from a tree just in front of him but Curtis had made it into the jungle. *Two*. The boom of .357 made Curtis look back and he saw Marshall standing. The return shot went high. *One*. Curtis drew the knife from his belt and crept forward through the trees.

Tammy was looking out to sea when Marshall fired. She turned at the sound.

"Did you get him?"

Marshall wiped sweat mixed with blood from his eyes.

"I don't know."

A shot whistled over their heads and Marshall winced.

"Guess not."

He re-sighted along the barrel at the place where he had seen the shadow of their assailant but could see nothing.

"Will…"

Marshall ignored Tammy and continued to scan the trees. The smallest of movements caught his eye through the leaves and he fired.

"Will."

"What is it?" he asked turning away from the jungle and ducking low.

"Is that, is that a ship? Tell me I'm not mad, Will. Please."

Marshall screwed up his eyes as he looked to the horizon. At first he saw nothing but as he tracked along he saw it. Something big and far out. A container ship or maybe a tanker.

"Jesus, it is."

Tammy fell to her knees.

24.

Curtis ducked behind a tree and then peeked around it. The man moved from his position and into some bushes to the left; he was small, maybe five four, and his grey hair was receding. No beard or stubble and for a moment Curtis wondered whether he shaved with the sword that was tucked through his belt. The man had one pistol shot left and the undrawn sword. Curtis looked down at the knife in his hand and it felt awfully inadequate. Looking around Curtis found a fist sized rock and hefted it into his hand. He hurled the rock and it crashed into the bushes a few metres from the man. He turned and fired the last round and Curtis was already running.

The man turned and watched Curtis sprinting towards him, knife held low. He made no move to draw the sword. Curtis tried to slow down but he was moving full pelt and came at the man in a rush. At the last moment the man pivoted on his front foot and performed a one hundred and eighty degree turn before firing out his leg in a side kick. Despite Curtis trying to back pedal the man's heel cracked against his chin and snapped his head back. Curtis stumbled to the right and tasted blood. He stayed on his feet and lashed out with the knife. The man stepped back out of his reach and still made no move for the sword.

When the man came forward it was fast. Curtis threw up his left to knock away a punch but the man pulled back the feint and put a kick into his stomach that knocked Curtis to the ground. He rolled clear as the man stamped a kick down at him and managed to stumble to his feet. Grabbing a branch Curtis threw it and watched as the man's arms became a blur and the sword seemed to leap into his hands before the branch was cleaved in two. They stood and faced each other, barely moving, watching. The man had the sword held out low and pointing behind him, he adjusted his grip and raised the blade, two-handed, above his head. Curtis could see the laughter in the man's eyes and knew he didn't have a chance.

"Curtis!"

The shout was close. The laughter fell away from the man's eyes and he shuffled forward. Curtis back-stepped and shouted.

"Here!"

There was a crashing through the bushes. The man lunged and Curtis danced back.

"You're fucked now."

The man looked at him and Curtis forced a smile, made a pistol with his fingers and pointed it at the man.

"Bang bang you little fucker."

The crashing grew closer and the man took a side step, then another and then ducked into the trees. Marshall and Tammy appeared a moment later, machete in Tammy's hand while Marshall held the empty .357 and a broken paddle from the raft.

"Was he here?" asked Tammy.

Curtis sat down in the dirt and pushed his fists into his eyes. He looked up at her and nodded.

"There's a ship."

"What?"

Marshall nodded.

"Looks like a tanker or something – far out but…"

Curtis looked towards the mountain top.

"The beacon."

"Is there time to rebuild it?" asked Marshall.

Curtis nodded.

"Yes, as long as we can get up there quickly. There're two flares in my rucksack. Better than nothing."

"Will they still work after they got wet?" asked Tammy.

Curtis smiled.

"Yeah, they will – waterproof, survival jobs."

Marshall laughed.

"Well, that's what we've got here isn't it – a survival job?"

*

The shame hangs on me like the sign on a hanged criminal. I had him, the yellow haired gaijin, *and should have taken his head. I let my pride override my duty. It will not happen again. They are running back for the mountain top, my peak. I have seen the ship as they have and cannot allow them to signal it. I am tired and the wounds ache, those in my soul as well as those in my flesh. I need to rest, to sleep. I would sleep a thousand years if I could and still rise to slay the enemies of my Emperor.*

*

Sweat poured off them as they climbed and mosquitoes buzzed around them. Curtis tried to keep his eye out for traps and snares but the tiredness clung to him like the ball attached to a cartoon convict's ankle. Marshall reached out a hand grabbed his shoulder.

"Are you okay?"

Curtis shook his head.

"I have to be, let's push on."

"Let me take point at least."

Curtis nodded and Marshall moved ahead.

Tammy caught up to Curtis and he nodded at Marshall.

"Maybe the asshole isn't such an asshole after all…"

She laughed.

"And he's still a fucking good photographer."

They continued on, Tammy helping Curtis to stay on his feet while Marshall scouted through the trees ahead. Marshall disappeared from view for a moment.

"Over here there's a trail, looks clear."

"No!" shouted Don but it was too late. As they ran towards Marshall's shout they heard the scream.

"Shit," swore Curtis as he drew his knife.

The trail that Marshall had found was obvious and inviting; cut through the jungle and the floor of it a carpet of grass. Marshall lay on the ground ahead of them with his arms outstretched. He screamed again as they got closer. Curtis saw the tripwire stretched across the trail that had knocked Marshall's feet from under him, as he fell he had put his hands out to break his fall and gone through a carpet of woven grass to land on to more sharpened stakes.

"Watch the jungle."

Tammy nodded and gripped the machete even tighter. Curtis went down on his knees and checked Marshall. The stakes had stabbed all the way through both of his hands and several of them had punctured his forearms. Marshall's face was a roadmap of pain; contour lines deep in his forehead, roads of agony dripping down his cheeks. As with the trap that had gotten Joelle the stakes were stained brown with filth.

"Will, I need to get you up off these. We have to get up to the beacon."

Marshall bit his lip and nodded. Curtis put his knife away and got in behind Marshall.

"This is going to hurt, I'm sorry but there's no other way."

Curtis gripped Marshall's wrists and tried to pull his arms up as carefully as possible. A scream tore from the photographer's throat. Curtis continued to lift, ignoring the sucking sounds from the wounds. Marshall pushed up with his knees, helping, and finally he was free. The blood that flowed from his wounds was thick and dark. Curtis tore his shirt in two and bound it tightly around Marshall's hands and arms.

"It'll have to do till we reach the peak."

Marshall gasped.

"Never. Felt. Pain quite like this."

"It's a shitter, isn't it?" replied Curtis "you just have to bite it down and try and remember a time when it didn't hurt."

Marshall nodded.

*

They carried Marshall between them, Tammy and Curtis, keeping his hands raised to try and slow the flow of blood from the wounds. After twenty minutes Curtis was ready to drop. They laid Marshall down and Curtis looked at Tammy.

"You'll have to go on."

"What? Don, no."

"Yes. It's the only way. He shouldn't be moved and I'm running on empty."

Curtis pointed to his rucksack which Tammy wore.

"The flares are in there," Curtis passed across his lighter "take that for the beacon. You get it lit then you light the flares and try to signal the ship. Do it as long as you can and then get back down here."

"What about *him*?" she said pointing at the jungle.

Curtis shrugged.

"If he comes he comes. I'll have to try and deal with him."

Tammy looked unsure.

"You have to go, Tammy. That ship is the only hope for any of us."

"Okay," she took a deep breath and looked Curtis in the eye "I want to get out of here, want us to get out of here."

Curtis gave her a weary smile and then kissed her.

25.

"Wish we had a smoke each?"

A grunt in response.

"Couple of cold beers."

Marshall laughed this time and it was a horrible sound. Curtis continued to sharpen the tip of the long branch he had found in the bushes. He had propped Marshall up against a tree. Curtis risked a look at the makeshift bandages around Marshall's arm. The blood was soaking through them.

"Thirsty?"

A weak nod and Curtis put the canteen up to Marshall's lips and gave him the last of the water.

"Shit, we're going to need more water. I'm going to see if there's a stream nearby."

"Urrrrgn. Don't. Please, don't leave me."

"I'm not going far, Will. We need the water or we aren't going to last long."

Marshall didn't have the strength to argue and he sagged back against the trunk of the tree. Taking the makeshift spear with him Curtis stepped into the bushes and moved forward on his guard.

*

Tammy moved slowly and carefully, jogging where she could but her eyes always on the lookout for anything that seemed out of place. She tried to watch like she had seen Curtis do when they moved up the trail before. The concentration of it was draining and she wondered how Don had managed to keep it up for so long. She stopped for a moment and drank from her canteen, wiping the sweat from her forehead with the back of her hand.

After she had clipped the canteen back to her belt Tammy took off at a quicker pace. She threw looks up at the peak. When she tripped on the vine tied between two trees she had to bite back a scream. She pulled away from where she almost landed, fearing another stake pit, and stayed low on the ground for almost a minute expecting a tree trunk to fall on her or spears to fire out from some hidden trap. Nothing happened and slowly her breath slowed and she climbed up onto one knee. She followed the vine over which she had tripped. It led into a thick bush. She pulled back the leaves and once more her breath became rapid and ragged, the sweat between the V of her breasts turning cold; a grenade had been bound to the tree, the pin was out of it. She waited for it to explode and tear her to shreds but it did nothing except remain impotent. A dud, she realised and got back to her feet. She headed off once again into the trees, moving more carefully now. When she had gone another fifty yards she felt and heard the low thump of an explosion. Her heart pounded like a death drum and bile rose in her throat. She spat the yellow mess into the dirt and pushed on.

*

The sound of the distant explosion snapped Curtis' head up. He had been filling the canteen in a small spring.

"Tammy!" he cursed himself for being weak and letting her head off alone.

Something caught his eye as he turned; amongst the trees a pile of stones and logs that didn't look natural despite the foliage draped over it. He re-attached the canteen to his belt, took up his spear and approached the small structure like a caveman heading into the cave of a great bear. The stones and logs had been placed over a dug-out pit about half a meter in depth. Inside was a blanket, an old munitions box and, to Curtis' surprise, a rifle that he recognised. He picked up the Arisaka that was missing its bolt and forced out the stripper clip. There were four rounds left in it.

It took Curtis a couple of minutes to free the jam. He replaced the bolt that he still had in his pocket, and put back in the feeder clip. He made a quick search of the dug-out but found no more ammunition. Hurling aside the sharpened stick he headed back for Marshall with the rifle cradled in his arms.

*

Marshall heard the explosion and looked up in the direction that Tammy had taken. He looked down at his ruined hands. *Don't think about it,* he told himself, *there's a ship. We're going to get out of here.* A rustling in the bushes made him look up.

"Don?"

His look turned to fear as he watched the small man step carefully out of the bushes. He looked at the katana in his hands and tried to get up. The man approached and shook his head. Marshall stopped trying to get up. The blade of the sword touched the nape of his neck and pushed his head forward.

Marshall stared at the dirt.

"I don't want to die."

He risked a look sideways but the man's face was like stone. Marshall thought about the others and the nature of their deaths, the butchery that had been inflicted upon them. *I'd rather it was clean.* Marshall leaned forward and offered his neck.

"Fuck you, you slant eyed bastard – do it!"

The man's face stayed impassive. Marshall looked away and then stared again at the dirt. He watched a worm moving in the earth and had time to see one tear drip onto the flesh of the creature before the blade fell.

*

As Marshall's head bounced away from the rest of him Curtis stepped out from the bushes.

"Shit!"

He brought the rifle to his shoulder and aimed at the central mass of the man – right between the buttons of his worn jacket. The man looked up and Curtis fired. The bullet hit him in the chest and knocked him down. Curtis worked the bolt and aimed again but the man was up and scuttling for the bushes like a crab.

"Not this time."

Curtis set off in pursuit.

26.

The shot echoed up to Tammy as she passed the ruins. She looked back trying to decide who could be firing. She knew that all Don and Will had was the empty revolver. She stood for a moment undecided about whether to continue up to the peak or head back down and try to help. The beacon had to be relit. It had to if they were to stand any chance of getting off the island. She turned and moved past the ruins. With the machete she hacked down branches, saplings and anything she could drag behind her. She remembered what Curtis had said when they first lit the beacon and stuffed handfuls of leaves into her pockets. And then she was out onto the black soil and dark volcanic rock.

The remains of the beacon were where they had left them. Tammy piled the branches and twigs atop the charred remains of their signal fire. She stuffed leaves where she could and then turned the wheel on the Ronson. She blew gently on the flame and waited till it took before lighting up another section. When it was alight she looked it and realised how small it was in the vastness. Their only hope was the smoke. She ran back down to the jungle, falling in her haste, and grabbed up more leaves from the ground which she placed on the fire. Once the smoke was pouring up she cracked one of the flares and stood in front of the beacon waving the red flame towards the far ship.

*

His quarry was fast but Curtis followed steadily in the man's wake confident that the Japanese would avoid his own traps. Curtis ducked low beneath a vine-covered branch and saw the man ahead. He smiled and moved off to the left. He watched a gap between two trees and as soon as the man moved into it he fired. Curtis couldn't be sure if his shot had been true or not. He moved forward to check and pulled himself to a halt. Beyond the trees lay a wide clearing filled with knee high grass. There were a couple of trees in the centre of the clearing, the only cover except for the grass itself.

Bringing the rifle up Curtis looked over the iron sights and tracked, looking for movement. He saw nothing. He switched position to where he could see the trees from another angle – there it was, a flash of the uniform jacket that the man wore, faded green-grey. Two shots left, Curtis slipped into the grass like a swimmer into a warm sea and ducked below the surface. He bellied forwards as gently as he could so as not to show his position with the sway of the grass, the rifle cradled across the crooks of his elbows.

He risked a glance over the grass. Closer to the trees now. He could see the hunched back, blood on the jacket. He bellied his way closer moving like a cautious snake closing in on its prey. Curtis expected the man to move, to run, to break for the trees but he remained where we was crouched amongst the trees. After checking the sights on the rifle Curtis stood and aimed straight at the back of the jacket. He fired once and quickly chambered the next round. Something was wrong. The bullet hadn't struck the way it should. Curtis fired again, knowing it was his last round. Again the strange flapping of the jacket and it was then Curtis realised his mistake – there was nothing in the jacket except for a couple of branches tied into a cross with a piece of vine.

The ground erupted next to Curtis as the man came out of hiding beneath his grass rug. The katana flashed and it bit into Curtis – straight into his gut. He screamed and batted the man across the face with the rifle barrel. The man turned and twisted the blade and Curtis screamed. The blade cut through flesh and Curtis heard the ripping as he was opened up. He bit down on the pain and with a roar lashed the rifle barrel once again across the man's face.

"Gonna kill you, bastard!"

The Japanese fell away and Curtis made to move in on him with the empty rifle. The pain he felt as he moved made stars burst before his eyes and his legs sway. He looked down; too much red, purple and brown of his intestines showing, a rainbow of hurt.

"Ah, shit, shit…"

Curtis stumbled away. The man looked up with blood smeared around his mouth from a broken nose. He watched as Curtis dropped the rifle and grasped his hands to his torn stomach. The man followed for a moment considering whether to take Curtis' head but when he saw the amount of blood that trailed from him he left him and walked back and collected the rifle, his rifle. The *gaijin* would die in his own time

*

Tammy waved the flare until the lactic acid burned in her shoulder and elbow, she switched arms and continued. Dusk was beginning to darken the sky and she hoped that it would help to carry the light of the beacon and the flare. She watched the tiny shape on the horizon until the dark obscured it from her.

She tossed the remnants of the flare to burn itself out in the dirt. The second flare stayed in the backpack. There was nothing else to do but head back down and find Don. She heard the grunting and then the heavy breaths coming from the dark towards the ruin. The machete was in her hand in a second. She held it two-handed and waited by the light of the fire.

It took moments for her to realise that it was Don shambling towards her. She threw her hand up to her mouth. She could see from the way he walked and held his hands tight to his stomach that something was badly wrong.

"Oh, Don. What has he done to you?"

He took a hand away from his gut and held it up, stumbled a few more steps and then his legs turned to rubber and he dropped into the dirt. She ran to him and pushed his hands away from his stomach. The torn flesh and ruined insides made her look away. Instead she looked at his face. So pale that it seemed luminescent.

"Baby, baby what happened?"

"Nearly got him. I'm sorry."

Curtis coughed and blood spilled over his lip. She stroked his hair.

"Will?"

"Dead, bastard cut his head off. Did the ship turn?"

"I can't tell."

A gurgle sounded from Curtis' throat. He coughed and then spoke again.

"I'm sorry. Sorry I couldn't have killed him, sorry I won't get to see how we would've turned out."

"It would have been good, Don. We would have been so good."

He smiled and his teeth were stained red.

"It would. I know it. Spent my whole life waiting for you and now I'm gone."

"No. Don, no you have to stay with me – don't leave me on my own, please."

"Can't, baby. You get down to the beach, the ship's coming I know it. I'm sorry. So sorry. Going now."

"No, no you're not. We are getting off this island and you're coming back to California with me. I want you to meet my parents, tell them about Vietnam so they know what it was like for my brother. I want you with me when I fall asleep and for you to still be there when I wake up. There's so much I want to show you and for you to show me. You can't go, Don. Not yet, please."

But Curtis was silent, still. Tammy stared down at him and then leaned in and kissed his still warm lips. She felt the wet on her cheeks and tried to sniff back her tears. She laid him carefully back down on the ground and reached for the machete. Her hand closed on the hard handle and her eyes grew harder still.

27.

The pain is exquisite and I can taste death within it. The blonde gaijin *was the wielder of death even though he is dead himself – there is a certain poetry in that and one which I can appreciate. If I had the strength I would write him a haiku. I have packed moss into the wound and bound it tightly. There is one yet on my island that seeks death and in the dark I will take it to her.*

*

The paths through the trees were dark and shadowed so Tammy stepped carefully picking each footfall before it touched the ground. If the ship was coming it would come to the beach. She had decided that she would head to the beach and use the last flare. The machete was tight in her fist and as she walked she tightened her heart against thinking of the man she had left dead back on the mountain. He was a good man and he shouldn't have had to die the way he did.

She looked up and moonlight lit the path ahead. It was clear. She thought of the dead, named them in her head; Don, Will, Nubia, Carmine, Heidi, Joelle, Francesca, Benjamin, Tony, Samson, Christopher, Gilbert. Tears tried to well in her eyes but she forced them back and looked up again. A shadow stood in the moonlight, sword long in its hand. Tammy stopped and raised her chin towards the figure. *So this is what death looks like*, she thought. The man moved slowly. *You hurt him, Don, you hurt him bad; maybe bad enough that I can get past him. Thank you.* She waited with the machete at her side. When the man was a few steps away he raised his sword. Tammy mirrored him with the machete. She watched him, saw the dark stains on his jacket.

With a sudden burst of speed he brought the sword up and slashed down at her head. Tammy parried the blow with the machete and danced to the side. He circled her and then her back was to the beach. So close. Not close enough. With a grunt Tammy launched herself forward throwing a hack at the man's head. He brought the sword up and the blades clashed. The man's feet moved quickly as he pushed the machete up and lanced his blade into Tammy's flank. She screamed as the razor sharp metal sliced through flesh and she jumped back. He smiled. Suddenly she turned and made a break for the beach. Pushing himself, he followed despite the protestations of his wounded body. When Tammy stopped and sliced out with the machete he had no time to stop or bring up his own blade. The machete bit into the flesh of his thigh. Tammy yanked the blade across and skipped away.

They stood bleeding, watching each other.

When he moved it was fast, despite his wounds, the blade of his sword dipped low and when Tammy dropped the machete to block it the blade danced up and made to kiss her throat. She threw herself back and ended up in the dirt. He stepped forward and slashed down at her. Just in time she got the machete in the way and sparks flew as the blades kissed. She kicked out and connected with his knee. The man dropped back looking at her the way a hunter watches a piece of dangerous, wounded, prey.

Tammy climbed up into a crouch and pointed the machete at the man. He watched, sword by his side. He came forward again. *Clang clang* as she blocked and then the blade of his sword caressed the flesh of her shoulder and opened it up in a dark fresh blossom.

He'd kill her, she knew it. Tammy took a step back and then another. The man followed up and held his sword high waiting for the killing blow to show itself. Tammy looked at him, breathed out through her nose, and hurled the machete. It span through the dark and the man dived away from the heavy spinning blade. It smashed away into the bushes off the trail and the man stood, a smile playing on his lips. Tammy smiled back and snapped the last flare alight. It glowed red in the night and she shoved it straight into the man's face. He screamed and Tammy smiled.

"Die you fucker!"

Flesh sizzled and the jelly of his eye tissue turned to liquid. Tammy twisted the flare, pulled it out and shoved it back into the man. His jacket caught fire and he screamed again. Dropped his sword and ran for the dark, a human torch illuminating his own path. Tammy kept hold of the bubbling flare and walked down to the beach. She waved the flare as soon as her feet touched the sand and kept waving it as she fell to her knees.

*

Tammy couldn't tell if the ship had turned or if any help was coming – it was just too dark. She stayed on her knees on the sand until flare was little more than a fist sized tube leaking red. She threw it up the beach and remained where she was.

She knew he was there without turning around. She could smell his burnt skin. He stood there, flesh smoking in the night and raised the katana. A sob wracked through Tammy's body but she wouldn't turn around. She stared straight ahead at the jet black see and thought of Captain Don Curtis – *I'll see you soon, Don.*

The blade moved like quicksilver in the night. Her head left her body and thudded into the sand. He watched her body for a moment until it toppled sideways and then nodded to himself. His island was his own once more.

Epilogue

The long boat hit the beach with the dawn. A dozen bored sailors climbed out of the boat onto the sands. They were mainly Filipinos but there was a smattering of Europeans and Americans amongst them. The first mate, a burly German, wore a .45 Colt in a hip holster and a couple of the crewmen held rifles that had been old when their fathers were born. The rest wore knives on their waists or carried iron bars.

They walked the beach and it wasn't long before one of the sailors found a wooden crate. He broke the top off and saw the bottles inside. The first mate was called over and smiled at the contents.

"Better signal the Captain. Best we camp here and look for whoever lost this," he gave an exaggerated wink as he spoke and the crew laughed.

*

Wounded as I am, I watch them. If they think they can come and take my island they are sorely mistaken. None of them seem to have the character of the blonde gaijin *or the woman who took my eye.*

I fight on, for honour – something that my countrymen discarded when they surrendered; something that you forgot when you went along with it. Unless you followed the correct path away from the shame and already await me on the other side of the veil. It matters little. I will see you again one day. One day soon, my love. Until then I wait with death, I wait with my island and I will not tolerate interlopers.

I cannot see them as well as I once did but it is the island that will do most of my killing for me, as always.

If you enjoyed *Slaughter Beach* then why not read Ben's new collection of weird westerns *Ride the Dark Country?* The book will be out soon in print and electronic versions from Dark Minds Press and to whet your appetite, here's an extract from one of the stories featured in the collection, *The Arroyo of the Worm*...

The rider was tall and sat high in the saddle on the Palomino; he was tanned by the southern sun but his eyes were light, he wore a planter's hat with a white shirt and tan riding breeches, a pistol was belted at his waist and a pair sat in scabbards ahead of the saddle. A pack horse trailed behind him at the end of a long bridle. The few residents of the pueblo, old men along with some young children and a few women, stared as he rode in. The rider drew the Palomino to a halt. An old man with a shock of white hair and a thick beard stood and walked over to the stranger.

"Hola, senor."

The rider nodded.

"You have ridden from the south?"

"Down near Veracruz."

"Guns and death I suppose."

"A whole heap of that."

"Senor, if you want money Maximilliano's men took it, if you want animals the Juaristas took them and if you want women the bandits took them. But we can offer you tortillas, beans and perhaps a little pulque."

The tall rider held down his fist and the old man reached to shake it only to find himself with a handful of silver coins.

"I'm William Gatlin, late of the army of the Confederate states and before that Front Royal, Virginia."

"They call me, Paco."

"Paco, from the wagons tracks running along that road yonder I'm reckoning that a party came down that road a few days back. Would I be right?"

"Si, four wagons and a few horses came from the south like you. Americans who said they were from *Carlota*."

Gatlin nodded and slid down from the saddle.

"How many days?"

"Three."

"My horse needs water and I could go for a jug of that pulque myself."

Paco clapped Gatlin on the shoulder and led him to a table beneath a canopy which hung from an adobe building that had seen better days. Flies buzzed around the table.

"No tables inside?"

A look of worry slid over Paco's features.

"Senor Gatlin there are two men inside, they are not good men. It is best you stay out here I think."

Two scabby horses, a flea bitten grey and a worn down dun were tied to post outside, and Gatlin looked at them while Paco patted the chair.

"Paco, I never did like flies in my tortillas."

He pushed open the door and stepped into the dark.

The cantina was dirt floored and the only light came a few candles scattered around on the tables. Two men sat at a table with clay cups of milky pulque in front of them. They looked over their shoulders as Gatlin stepped inside. The two men wore straw sombreros with wide brims; one was pock marked with a wall eye, the other rat featured with a thin moustache – both wore large horse pistols on their hips.

"Hola," offered Gatlin.

The men turned in their seats and sneered.

Gatlin took a seat at an empty table across the room from the two men. A girl appeared, she was young but Gatlin could see the swellings of womanhood beneath her cheap dress. The shoulder of her dress was torn and the two men laughed as she stayed as far away from them as the tables would allow. She placed a clay cup before Gatlin. Her eyes showed fear. Gatlin took a mouthful from the cup and then put it back on the table. The man with the pockmarked face rose and walked across the rooms, spurs jangling with each step.

"You didn't finish it, senor."

"I know the custom."

"So why didn't you finish it, gringo?"

"Perhaps I didn't consider the company worthy of the custom."

The man's hand jerked towards the Colt Dragoon at his waist. Gatlin raised his hand.

"Could be I spoke a little hastily allow me a chance to finish it."

Gatlin upended the clay cup into his mouth, watching all the time as the man closed his hand around the grip of his pistol. The first bullet took the man through his wall eye the second through his chest. Gatlin stood up with the cup still pressed to his lips his Beaumont-Adams revolver aimed straight and shot the second man through his mouth. Placing the cup on the table he crossed the dirt floor and fired a shot through the man's heart.

"I'll take those tortillas and beans now."

Made in the USA
Charleston, SC
02 July 2016